Must Love Christmas

Must Love Christmas

A Montana Bachelors and Babies Romance

Kelly Hunter

TULE
PUBLISHING

Chapter One

"MORNING, LILA." MADELINE Love, only offspring of Wall Street moneymaker Jonas Love, tried to glide rather than rush toward the skyscraper's bank of private elevators. "Is it midday yet?"

"Two minutes to go." The elevator doors opened, and Lila put out her arm to keep them that way until Madeline got in. "Great outfit. Love those colors on you."

"You think so? I try." She always tried to look her best when meeting her father. Today she wore suede boots and a matching skirt in the exact same caramel color as her eyes. She'd added an ivory silk shirt with an off-center bow at the neck and topped it with a lightweight cashmere coat in Persian blue. Her coat ended just above her skirt and the slender cut made the most of her slight curves. "My father's taking me out to lunch, fingers crossed."

The doors closed on Lila's, "Good luck."

Knees and heels together, Madeline leaned forward to check her appearance in the mirrored wall. She tidied her silky auburn waves as best she could before leaning closer and checking her teeth for lipstick. By the time the lift doors opened she was a picture of hopeful serenity.

She wasn't late. She was right on time.

The lift opened into her father's outer reception area and the first person she saw was her father's loyal executive secretary. "Good morning, Symonds."

"Happy birthday, Miss Madeline." He gestured to an enormous bouquet of peonies peppered with whimsical greenery. "Don't forget to pick up your flowers on the way out."

"You never forget. And you always remember the flowers I like best. Is he free?"

"He's free." But she hadn't taken more than two steps toward the door of her father's inner sanctum before Symonds stopped her with a word. "Coat."

Symonds had already emerged from his side of the reception desk to help her wriggle her way out of it. Which meant she then had to smooth everything down and tidy her hair all over again. "How do I look?"

"Pretty as a picture, as always."

She didn't believe him, but he was a dear sweet man who always made her feel welcome, even when she wasn't. She raised her hand and knocked on the door and waited. Her father wouldn't open the door for her, he never did, but Symonds moved into position, grasping the door handle, ready to proceed on cue.

"Come in."

And... enter the billionaire's daughter, on time, on task,

and manicured to perfection.

"Madeline." He didn't rise from his seat behind the glossy executive desk to greet her. He never did, her silver fox of a father with his rangy physique, piercing blue eyes, and air of ruthless command.

"Dad." She offered what she hoped was a sunny smile.

"Happy birthday."

"Thank you. It feels good to be twenty-five." Not that she'd done all that much with her life to date but her interior design career was steadily progressing, and she was learning a lot and had proper friends for what felt like the first time in her life.

He nodded. "Good, good. Do you remember the ranch in Montana?"

"Yes." Did he seriously think she was likely to forget it?

"It's yours."

"I'm sorry? I don't understand. I didn't even know you still had it."

"It passed to you when your mother died, and by the terms of her will, it's been held in trust until you turned twenty-five."

"But…" There were still all kinds of gaps in her comprehension. "You've never mentioned *any* kind of inheritance from my mother."

"You were a child at the time."

"Yes." *At the time.* "But children grow up. Why didn't you ever mention it?"

His blue eyes narrowed as if she'd somehow disappointed him, but that was nothing new. She'd realized years ago that her father found parenting a challenge. He'd supported her financially, no question. But he'd pretty much outsourced any other kind of parental role.

He pushed a bulging folder across the desk. "The Serenity Valley ranch is yours free and clear with no taxes owing. The grazing land has been leased to neighboring ranchers over the years and that lease is due for renewal this January. The same neighbors also periodically offer to purchase the place for above market price. I suggest you accept. The house needs maintenance. Ask Symonds to put you in touch with my solicitors if you need more information."

"I… thought we were going for lunch?"

"Something's come up."

"Oh." It usually did. She hid her disappointment with well-practiced ease. Her father was a very busy man. "I don't know what to say. Thank you?"

For holding onto her legacy even if he'd kept her in the dark all these years?

For not once saying, *Hey, remember the ranch? It's going to be yours one day so keep that in mind as you plan out your life and continue to exist far, far away from me.*

She folded her arms across her middle and then just as quickly dropped them, knowing her pose would come across as defensive. "I mean, yes, of course, thank you for caring for it all this time. I'm a little overwhelmed. But thrilled," she added. "Definitely thrilled."

"I'd have sold it years ago and built you a far more profitable asset portfolio, but you have to understand that my hands were tied by the terms of the will."

"But money isn't everything." Possibly not the smartest thing to say to a man who had dedicated his life to conquering the money market and thoroughly succeeded. She reached for the folder. Her mother's gift from beyond the grave. "I have such good memories of the ranch."

"I didn't think you would." How cool he sounded, but for the small catch in his throat at the very end.

"Well." Traumatic memories threatened to overwhelm her as she dropped her gaze to the table and tried to take an invisible breath. "Some of them I'd rather forget, but not all. Maybe I'll spend Christmas there this year and make better memories. Do you remember all the snow? And sledding down the hill behind the house? And the round sunken lounge and the fireplace and the little town nearby? What was its name again? Marietta?" She hurried on, words tumbling because his attention never failed to make her nervous. "You're welcome to join me there for Christmas if you can find the time?" Not that he would. He was a very important, very busy man, but she never stopped asking. Hope was her friend.

"Let's do it."

Shock left her speechless.

Her father sat back in his wingback leather power chair,

every inch the successful stock-market tycoon that he was. "Did you not just invite me to spend Christmas with you at the ranch?"

"Yes. Yes, I did." Probably not the time to remind him that he hadn't spent Christmas with her in years. With her father unavailable, and a family unit that consisted of just the two of them, she'd taken to riding out the delights of the season first at boarding school and then at the midtown loft her father had gifted her on her twenty-first birthday. But she'd always wanted to spend it with him. She hadn't given up hope. "It'll be so much fun."

"I'd like to bring some guests."

"Okay." She nodded, widened her eyes, and figured why not? Christmas was a time of giving. She didn't need all her father's attention. Just some of it. "Sounds good. Business associates?"

"My son."

Madeline blinked.

"He's seven. You'll need to get a tree in with all the trimmings."

"Your... *son*." Across all her expensive therapy and brutal self-examination when it came to why her father had all but abandoned her after her mother's death, him having another family to be with had never once crossed her mind. In the end, she'd been encouraged to think that far from him being neglectful, she was simply asking too much of a very busy man. "You have a son?"

"Yes."

"Who is seven." Saying it aloud did not increase her understanding. *"Who you've never mentioned?"*

"And my fiancée will be joining us as well."

"You have a fiancée?" Her fingers clenched over the back of a nearby chair. "Do you mind if I sit?"

"I have another meeting in five minutes."

She sat anyway, clasped her hands on top of the folder he'd just given her and squared her shoulders, legs crossed below the knee and knees together just so. This was what expensive finishing schools in Switzerland were good for, she realized suddenly. These moments when everything she thought she knew about her world had just been proven false… and there she sat, demurely attentive. Not one single scrap of her inner turmoil evident.

Or maybe she was dreaming, and her father could see full well that she was weeping existential angst all over the Aubusson.

"Your fiancée… is the… your son's mother?" Maybe her father had been with this woman briefly eight or so years ago and then something had happened to part them, and… "And you've probably only just found out you have a son and…"

"No."

"Oh." She had no other words to put toward this situation.

"I was there at Cade's birth."

"Oh." Her half-brother had a name.

"I usually spend Christmas with Cade and his mother."

A mother who apparently did not have a name.

"Irene married a financier earlier this year and is choosing to holiday with her new husband this festive season so it's my turn to have Cade for Christmas."

Irene. Cade. Irene had a husband now. He probably had a name too.

Her father's lips twisted in a bitter little grimace and Madeline stared, fascinated. Who was this man in her father's office, wearing his face and using his voice to say all these words she didn't understand? "Rebecca, my fiancée, has expressed interest in meeting my children and I've been telling her about passing the ranch over to you. She's never been to Montana and said she'd like to go there one day if she can clear her patient schedule. Many birds, one stone."

No kidding. "Patient schedule, you said. So, she's a...?"

"Cardiac surgeon."

Of course she was. Her father would never be satisfied with someone mediocre.

"I trust you can make provisions for us all?" Her father was standing, dismissing her, ready or not, as he strode to the door. "We'll fly in on Christmas Eve and leave on the twenty-eighth."

"Of course." *Concentrate on the little things like walking without stumbling off the floor rug.* Wasn't as if it was a cliff. Hey, look, she did it, shoulders back and standing tall at just under six foot in chunky-heeled boots. But as she got to the door he held open for her, brutally polite as always, she paused and met him directly eye to eye. "I have a seven-year-old half-brother and you never thought to mention him until now?"

"It seemed prudent not to."

"Prudent." Granted she wasn't always the most rational Barbie doll in the toy chest—she'd needed therapy after her mother had died, but that was going back over a dozen years ago now. She'd been eleven at the time and fragile after witnessing her mother's passing, but so what? She wasn't fragile now, and she had a big heart. "Prudent how?"

"Judicious."

"I know what the words *mean*. Wise. Careful. Discreet. I just don't know how to apply them to you not telling me you have another family. Did you think I wouldn't fit in? Wouldn't accept a new sibling? Wouldn't want to be part of your new family unit?" *Don't you know me at all?* "I would have *loved* to be part of all that." Sure as shit beat going through life alone.

"Now, Madeline. Don't be like that."

Like *that*? Like *what* exactly? Needy? Dependent? *His daughter?* Entitled to think he might share such information with her? "How long have you been engaged?"

He had the grace to look uncomfortable. "I met Rebecca two months ago. We got engaged last week."

Whirlwind romance. Not that she judged him, but...

okay, yes. Hefty, judgy judgment in progress.

"I am entitled to lead my own life, Madeline."

Yes, yes he was. And his relationship with her had been dysfunctional for years. Wasn't as if this was news.

"We can go elsewhere this Christmas if you no longer care to play host," her father was saying.

"No!" Dammit, what did it matter if he'd withheld important information from her for years? He was sharing it now and that was what counted. *Look forward, not back.* She could do that. "No, I can do it. I'd love to do it. I love Christmas, do you remember all the fun we used to have at the ranch?" That place had been such an entertainer's delight and could be again. "The more the merrier, right?"

He smiled and just for a moment she thought she saw the father she'd had when she was a little girl. The loving, laughing face of him before her mother had died, and he'd shut down completely.

"There is one more thing I want to ask of you, Maddie."

Maddie. The name he used to call her all those years ago. She beamed; she couldn't help herself. Always would when he reminded her of the love her world had once been so very full of.

"Any possessions of your mother's, any pictures, family photos. I want them gone."

Chapter Two

IN HINDSIGHT, MADELINE probably shouldn't have made plans to go back to work after her meeting with her father. She should have phoned her employer Bette and asked for the rest of the afternoon off. She shouldn't have rushed from her father's office without her birthday flowers, shouldn't have bought a slice of pizza and tried to eat it through her tears while perched on a bench in Bryant Park. That way she wouldn't have dropped an oily dollop of pepperoni and cheese onto her suede skirt. And, of course, she should have been watching where she was going on her long walk back to Bette's interior design salon. It would have saved her stepping in a pile of sticky, stinky muck.

Probably a minor miracle she hadn't been run over.

Let it go, Madeline. Just let all the shit he just piled on you go.

An inheritance from her mother.

A new fiancée.

A son.

Madeline, your father has intimacy issues. It's not you. It's him. He may still be processing the loss of your mother. Those were the words of the third child psychiatrist her father had charged with "setting her right." Words Madeline had clung to as she'd navigated her teenage years. Psychiatrist number one had been blunter and not exactly helpful at the time. *You have to understand that your father's a very busy man.* So much for all their fine words.

Her very important, very busy father hadn't been processing a devastating loss and hiding from intimacy at all. He just hadn't wanted to include *her*.

Anger was slowly encroaching on her earlier shock, even if sorrow kept its watch.

Own your situation, Madeline. Think your way through it and control what you can. The musings of child psychologist number two. Number two—a man—had called her father a delusional, self-serving coward.

To his face.

There'd been no more number two after that and Madeline had spent a good many years trying to erase number two's words from her mind, but they always came back.

What if, as part of this inheritance, her father had closed the door on the ranch and walked away and never looked back?

It'd be like a time capsule, taking her back to the last days her mother had spent on this earth and if that was the case, Madeline too might be on board with clearing some of those reminders away. Not all of them, screw her father's directive in that regard. But some.

Maybe his directive to clean the place up hadn't been as brutal as it sounded.

She'd been hoping to sneak in the back entrance to Bette Sanson Interiors and clean herself up before she hit the salon floor, but Bette had seen her hurrying past and beckoned her in the front entrance—which was how Madeline came to be standing cold-nosed and coat in hand, hiding her pizza stain as best she could as she attempted to explain to an old-money midtown matriarch why the midcentury Danish armchair in the window last week was no longer available.

The unavoidable fact that another customer had bought it didn't seem to register.

And Madeline, ordinarily the firm's most accomplished soother of difficult customers, seemed to have lost her touch, her care factor, and any patience she'd once possessed.

"I do know of chairs in that style that are coming up for auction." Madeline made one last attempt to appease the woman. "Let me pull them up on screen for you." No desktop computer screen for Bette's well-heeled clientele. Bette had a dedicated projector and a white wall that could render any image at full size with perfect clarity. Madeline moved behind the desk, grateful for the opportunity to hide her dirty boots, because no way Bette and the customer hadn't noticed or more to the point smelled them. "And then I really do need to excuse myself."

"I'm afraid I'm not interested in any other chair," said the woman with a sniff.

"Pity." Madeline pulled up the picture she'd been looking for anyway. "Because these are a pair of Wegner prototype occasional chairs in walnut with classic tan leather upholstery. They never went into production for the company and have been sitting under sheets in an Umbrian palazzo for the past sixty years." She pulled up another picture of the two, and then another. "I understand from the auctioneer that the reserve is quite reasonable. They truly are unique."

The client studied them with an air of reluctant interest. "Can you get them here for me to look at?"

"The chairs are for viewing in Rome. Here at Bette Sanson, we can and do bid at auction on behalf of our clients."

"So, the answer's no." Seemed like the older woman hadn't heard the word before.

"The answer's no," Madeline replied calmly. "We source, you buy. It's a business model that allows us the flexibility to accommodate whatever budget our clients are comfortable with." It also provided Bette some measure of protection against clients who continually changed their mind. Amazing how often that *didn't* happen when the clients were using their own money. "We're a full-service interior design team, though it seems you're not interested in having us do any design work for you. You're just after a chair. Am I right?"

Bette's bright smile had frozen in place. Madeline should probably plaster a smile on her face too at this point, but it was suddenly all too much.

The woman seemed to be trying to stare down her aquiline nose. Unfortunately, if she wanted to look Madeline in the eyes she had to look up. Way, way up. "You're a very blunt young woman. What's your name?"

"Madeline Love." She took a business card from the holder. "The auction house is Bonhams, you'll need to be online from fourteen hundred EDT tomorrow." She pushed the card across the deck, uncaring if the customer picked it up or not. "I'm delighted to bring the pair to your attention. I'm sure Bette will take very good care of you should you choose to pursue them through us. Beyond that, happy bidding and good luck."

No *excuse me*, she'd already tried that once.

She left without a backward glance and made her way through to the back room where the glamour and luxury of the front parlor made way for crammed functionality and filing cabinet after filing cabinet of design plans and brochures from suppliers. Bette had a list of preferred suppliers for everything from tap fixtures to drape makers to custom-made floor rugs, and Madeline was grateful to Bette for taking her on fresh out of design school and sharing her industry contacts and resources, but Madeline worked shockingly long hours in order to pull rabbits out of hats on a regular basis, and in all the time she'd worked here, she'd never had a raise and she'd never been put in charge of a job, not even a simple one.

She worked the showroom floor and placed orders for the gorgeous homewares that all the other designers and their clients had chosen. Day in, day out, no cardiac surgery involved.

She removed her offending boot and ran it under the tap in the industrial basin next to the staff bathroom. The suede was ruined but at least she could make sure the smell was gone by the time Bette cornered her. Nothing she could do about the stain on her skirt except go home, take it off, get it dry-cleaned and hope the cleaning staff were miracle workers who still wanted to be miracle workers at the end of a thankless day.

When she looked up, Bette stood in the doorway, arms crossed beneath her chest and a scowl on her face that made Madeline sigh. Offense was probably her best defense. "She was a time waster."

Bette's scowl deepened. "She was *old money.*"

"And short of using *your* money to buy and bring the chairs here so she could sit on them and say no, there was no pleasing her. I know this, you know this, she knew this. Did she arrange for us to bid on the chairs?"

"No."

"Time waster." There was no point scrubbing the side of her shoe any further. She ran it under the tap one last time and reached for a drying cloth.

"She did say she'd think about them though. And she did take your card."

"Bet she gets one of her own people to bid on them."

"When did you get so cynical?" Bette was eyeing her

with something that looked a lot like concern, her business-like persona replaced by a maternal one that made Madeline uncomfortable. "Because you left here looking like sunshine and now you look like someone stole your puppy. What happened with your father? He too busy to see you again?"

"No, that was last time. This time he gave me five minutes. I even took a seat. Very assertive. You'd have been proud of me." He'd shown her the door with unseemly haste, but progress was progress.

"Oh, doll. If you don't know that man's a waste of your precious time by now, I can't help you."

"Ditto on the old-money matriarch. But I'll mockup a sitting room window with those chairs in pride of place in case she does come back." She took a deep breath. "Bette, I just inherited a cattle ranch in Montana. I didn't even know we still had it—I thought it had been sold years ago, only it was mine all along and now I've turned twenty-five my father's handing it over, as per the instructions in my mother's will."

That about covered it.

"You stepped out for lunch with your father and inherited a ranch," echoed Bette. "How big a ranch?"

"Big. And a stunning ranch house to go with it and I do mean stunning." She reached for the folder and opened it to show Bette an exterior shot of the house.

"Holy cow, girl. What are you going to do with that?"

Good question. Great question. She had no idea. "I want

to see it again in person." That much she knew for certain.

"You could redesign the interior. Make it a showcase for your skills. Start your own business. Use it as a launch pad."

"Are you firing me?" Because the way this day was unfolding, that was next.

"Of course I'm not. Why would you think that?"

"Why would I think that? Bette, I've been here two years and you still haven't sent me out on a job! My color work is better than anyone else's here, I *balance* half the designs the other designers come up with before the client even sees them. I spend hours online looking for just the right pieces to go in a room and then you or one of the other designers come in and says, 'Ooh, they're nice, I'll have those for the Sommerville house,' and the client is thrilled, and the designer gets to add to their ever-growing resume, but where's my body of work? My project portfolio?" She'd never spoken to Bette like this before. Not once. "I know I didn't present well out there today. Too grubby, too curt, too damn much of me all up in the woman's space. I also know my design work could dazzle her and anyone else who comes in here if given the chance. *Are* you going to give me that chance?"

Bette frowned. "You want the truth?"

"Please. Because I don't know what I'm doing *wrong*, and if I don't even know that how on earth can I fix it?"

"Maddie, honey. Your work is exceptional. The only thing you need is confidence, and until today I've never seen you wear it. You're the most talented interior designer I know—and that includes me. Make no mistake, the moment I put you out for hire you're going to be in demand. From a business perspective, having you elevate our work from behind the scenes has been good for me and every other designer on my payroll, and I am, above all, a businesswoman. And before you think of me as utterly Machiavellian, I *don't* happen to think these last two years you've spent building relationships with suppliers and being understudy on a hundred jobs instead of lead designer on a few has been bad for you. You've had the experience without the pressure. You now know what can go right or so very, very wrong. You've had practice troubleshooting some of our most difficult clients—without the responsibility for the mistake in the first place." She held up her hand. "You're my protégé. What's more you have the money, connections, and social status to launch your own business any time you want. You have all the talent you need, and now"—she tapped the folder—"you have an asset most designers can only dream of. Why *wouldn't* you want to go and make that place scream Madeline Love Interiors—designer to the stars who want to be cowboys for a week or two every summer? Do it! Take this gift from your mother and *use* it."

Was Bette really suggesting she launch her own interior design platform? Now? At twenty-five years old and with a design degree in her back pocket, sure, but only two years in the business? "Er, Bette…? I don't—"

"And there it is," the older woman interrupted swiftly. "*You. Lack. Confidence.* And I don't know if that's your daddy's doing or someone else's or whether you come by your meekness naturally, but you need to bring on the brash and start believing in yourself and push *back* when people try to push you around. That's what I've been waiting to see in you before I let clients loose on you. *That*'s what I saw in you today. Stand up for yourself, Madeline. This is my advice to you. It's the only career advice you need."

It was kind of hard to take Bette's words as a compliment when the only reason Madeline had stood up for herself out in the showroom was because she'd already been pushed to breaking point by her father. Once she was more herself again would her natural inclination to bend to the will of others return? Or was that something she could try and change?

No more Madeline the people-pleasing pushover.

Hello Madeline, the savvy, successful interior designer in demand.

She tried to project an air of quiet certainty. "So, if I said I'd like to take some leave and explore my options in Montana, would you keep my position open for me so I can return if it doesn't work out?"

"No. That won't work for me. I need someone on the shop floor when I'm not. But what I can do is start bringing you on as a design consultant for specific projects. You get to keep your hand in, work from Montana and build your portfolio. I get to keep my hooks in you for a little while longer."

"That's…"

"Perfect?" suggested Bette.

"I was going to say scary."

"Not as if you need the money." Bette looked again at the picture of the ranch house. "Tell me more about this place?"

"It's in Montana in a gorgeous valley to the east of Marietta and with the Crazy Mountain range as a backdrop. The paperwork says it was bequeathed to my mother upon my grandmother's death, and then to me upon my mother's death, to be held in trust until I turned twenty-five. But my mother and grandmother died within months of each other when I was eleven and I had no idea it was mine until today." She didn't usually talk money with her coworkers, but figured she owed Bette the full picture. "Taxes are killer, but it looks like the income from leasing the grazing land helps with that and I can probably afford to keep it if I want to. It's big—nine bedrooms, five bathrooms, with a huge atrium in the central living area. Think stonework and timber interiors, deer antlers and not nearly enough windows to cut the gloom. Last time I was there it was full of midcentury designer furniture. It might still be full of it."

She took a deep breath. "Bette, we're talking shag rugs, orange and lime-green wallpaper, sunken lounge rooms, nonstop leather sofas, the lot. It's a shrine to the nineteen seventies."

"Please tell me that nonstop sofa is a *De Sede*."

"A hundred feet of it in burnt orange, that I crawled and draped all over as a kid, yes." It was worth the brag to see Bette's eyes light up with delighted mirth.

"Be still my heart. I want pictures. And first dibs on anything you don't want to keep."

Any possessions of your mother's, any pictures, family photos. I want them gone.

Her father's words. Not hers.

Not the feeling in her heart.

"My mother spent the last months, the last day of her life in that house and I was right there with her to the end. What if my father just pulled the door closed and walked away and nothing has changed?" She felt close to tears again, never mind the tears she'd shed at lunch.

"All the more to work with and love." Bette tracked her impending emotional breakdown with the ease of a woman who'd spent the last thirty years navigating New York retail. "Make a list of anything you think you'll need help with. Book your flights. Arrange for a car at the other end. Get the electricity connected if it isn't already. Make sure you have internet."

"You're bossy."

"And *call me* when you get there. I want daily updates on the treasures you unearth, and an invitation to come and see the place in person once you're done."

"What are you doing for Christmas?" Madeline was only half joking.

Within moments, Madeline found herself enveloped by five foot nothing and ninety pounds worth of steel-spined New Yorker, and it wasn't that she didn't like hugs. More that she hadn't had a mom hug for the past fourteen years, and, dammit, she was not about to let this one and Bette's support undo her. "Hugging," she squeaked. "Happy hugging. Are we done yet?"

Betty pulled back and favored Madeline with her brightest megawatt smile. "Darling, you've only just begun."

Chapter Three

I T WASN'T THE hat that made Seth Casey a cowboy at heart—even though he wore his proudly. It wasn't that he was the third son of five, or that he hailed from a well-respected ranching family or that the raising of cattle was second nature to him.

No, what made him a cowboy was the stubbornly independent streak that had landed him a carpentry apprenticeship at seventeen, much to the relief of his family who didn't have any ranch work left for their third son to see to.

What made him a cowboy was the try in him that had seen him start his own building company a year after he'd finished his apprenticeship. He'd been riding high on hope and swagger, with barely enough money to paint a sign on the door of his truck.

His two older brothers had called him reckless and figured he'd be broke within six months.

His youngest brother Jett—already a world champion downhill skier with sponsorship and endorsement deals on the rise—had asked Seth if he needed a silent partner to help with startup costs and Seth hadn't been too proud to accept the offer.

He'd taken the cash and his reckless cowboy confidence and built his company to the point where he now ran three summer crews in addition to the eight permanent employees he kept on year round. So far, the building game had been good to him.

These days he specialized in restoration and renovation work for the wealthy who came to Montana to buy a slice of ranching history. Why they then opted to renovate their ranch houses to resemble their Hollywood Hills mansions remained a mystery to him. He usually tried to talk them out of their more outlandish requests but when that didn't work he went all-in on giving them exactly what they asked for.

Who was he to argue about the glass-domed yoga tower the popular young actress wanted for her rustic log cabin? Had it looked beyond stupid by the time he'd finished building the tower to the L.A. architect's specifications? Yes. Would it fall down? No. The pretty movie star could do naked night yoga in her see-through dome and let her soul soar into the heavens and all the very best to her.

Unfortunately, his hard-won agreeableness had a habit of disappearing whenever he thought of the ranch house that sat empty and unkept five miles to the north of the Casey ranch he'd grown up on. You couldn't *leave* a house like that empty for years in this climate. Not and expect it to hold up to that kind of neglect. Even the actress with the yoga dome had caretakers come in to maintain her property in her absence.

But the Love place sat empty, slowly going to ruin, never mind its idyllic views and the best mix of sunlight and protection from the worst of the weather. Built by a Dane in nineteen twenty-eight—all sixteen thousand foot of it—and bought by the Loves in the late nineteen sixties, it needed the care and attention only a master craftsman and local inhabitant could give it.

The Love ranch might not belong to him, *yet*, but he'd been making offers on it for the past five years and one day Mr. Bigshot Wall Street Broker Jonas Love was going to sell it to him.

He'd taken a detour up to the ranch house on his way to work because the place had been calling to him again. Sure enough, a length of guttering had come loose, swinging in the wind next to a broken window. He'd ended up on a ladder and then on the roof, swearing up a storm as he dumped snow on the ground, determined not to think of his actions as trespassing as he hammered and drilled the warped and saggy guttering back in place and then set about boarding up the window.

It wasn't trespassing if there was no one there to see him.

It was more a matter of taking care of what would one day be his.

WHEN THE RENTAL car agency people at Bozeman airport assured Madeline that she'd need both snow tires on the vehicle and a set of chains in the back in order to get where she was going, she took their word for it. She'd never driven through Montana in October before, never driven on snow-plowed roads through a wonderland of snow-covered valleys and towering peaks. Even in Switzerland, at finishing school where she'd learned to drive among other things, she'd never felt quite this far from civilization.

She had half a mind to keep right on driving until she reached Marietta, but the public road into Serenity Valley had been freshly plowed and for some reason the driveway up to her ranch house had been plowed as well. Maybe someone from the electricity company had been out and that was why. Maybe she'd only have to shovel her way to the front door. The rental car people had given her a shovel to go with her snow chains and she hadn't known whether to be grateful or intimidated.

Madeline Love, mountain woman. Fully prepared for whatever Montana could throw at her. A confident, capable, and assertive career woman, striking out on her own.

She let her big, family-sized 4WD crawl to a stop behind a tradesman's truck and cut the engine. The music she'd been using to soothe her nerves stopped too. She reached for her new winter coat and wished she'd thought to bring better boots as she stepped from her ride and sank into snow past her ankles.

The lettering on the side of the work truck said CASEY CONSTRUCTION COMPANY. Not the North West electricity company, then, but the name was familiar. According to her father's folder full of paperwork she leased grazing land to Casey Pty Ltd.

A path had been cleared but it didn't lead to the front door, it went to one side of the house, where a guy up a ladder was boarding up a window. Judging by the lack of snow on a section of roof above him he'd also been up there as well.

She had no idea who he was, but she was already glad to see him. "Hello?"

He didn't turn around.

"Hey, up there."

Nothing.

But he finished drilling the board into place a short time later, and it was no trouble—absolutely no trouble at all—to wait and watch him while he worked. He had a confidence up that ladder that she knew she'd never be able to match and an economy of movement that spoke of power and control and no small measure of grace. He was a tall guy, built lean and rangy, and he wasn't wearing gloves. His hand made the power drill look small.

She waited until he'd finished what he was doing, and his boots hit the ground before trying again. No point scaring the man off the ladder if he thought he was the only one here.

"Hey!" She made her voice loud enough to be heard and this time he did turn. He took his time removing his gray knit beanie and earphones, and all the while his midnight gaze skewered her. Hand over heart, she'd never met anyone who could stop her breath with just a glance.

Until now.

"Hi," she said, a lot less forcefully and raised her hand in greeting, before hurriedly tucking her hands beneath her armpits because boy was it cold and she wasn't wearing gloves. Rookie mistake.

She wondered what his excuse was.

He cocked his head, a black-eyed, bed-headed son of outrageous beauty, blessed with the kind of easy confidence she didn't have a hope of matching.

"Hi." His voice matched the rest of him, a gruff and rumbling baritone that skittled along her nerve endings. He had a slightly crooked nose to go with his high cheekbones, strong jaw, and beautifully shaped lips. He waited, and she really should have spent less time ogling the man and more time figuring out what she wanted to say next, but in the end, he saved her the trouble. "Need any help? Cause you look a little lost."

Insta-lust probably did that to a person. Made them lose their way. "Oh. No, not lost. I'm right where I want to be." His eyes narrowed and she soldiered on. "I'm Madeline Love. My family"—no, that wasn't right—"I own this place."

Recognition flared in those obsidian eyes. "You're Jonas Love's daughter."

"Yes."

"Doesn't he own the ranch?"

"No. It's mine."

The guy in front of her narrowed his eyes. "Seth Casey. My family owns the ranch next door. I've been making offers to buy this place for years. Offers I've been sending to your father." He held out his hand in greeting.

Gingerly, she slid her hand in his, expecting it to be cold but it was warm. After one gentle clasp from his calloused, iron paw the handshake was done. She immediately wondered what it would be like to have the right to reach out and hold that hand any time she wanted.

For some reason she thought it might be nice.

"My father's been holding the ranch in trust for me, and I've only just met the age qualification and taken control," she said by way of answering a question he hadn't yet asked. "Does he employ you to maintain the house?"

"No one maintains the house." There was judgment in his voice, and she swallowed down an automatic apology. "I saw the gutter down as I drove past and decided to fix it. Your window's broken too. And don't take this the wrong way, but why own the place at all if you're just going to let it rot?"

Ouch. She didn't have an answer for him that wouldn't incriminate her father and expose her utterly dysfunctional family to his gaze. "So, what would you do with it if you took ownership?" she countered, offense being the best defense in this instance. "Do you have a family, Mr. Casey? A wife and children to fill up all those rooms?"

"Not yet," he replied easily. "But I do have a widowed mother who lives a few miles back, and I have four brothers, two older and two younger, all with strong ties to this part of the world. If you're asking me if I'd live in the place, look after it, and use it the way it should be used, the answer's yes."

"Oh." So… Good answer.

"What about you? You plan to live here now?" he asked.

"Does that not sound like a good idea?"

"Alone?"

"Y-es?" Why-oh-why did she have to sound so hesitant? Where was her fierce inner mountain woman? "I mean, *yes*. It's just me, although my father and others will be joining me for Christmas."

"You're here until Christmas?"

"Y-es." *Confidence, Madeline!* "I mean, *yes*."

He scratched his head and glanced at the house. "Don't take this wrong—aw, hell, you're going to take this wrong no matter how I say it—but now is not the time to start living here in the valley if you're not used to it. Summer, yes. Winter, no. Especially if you're by yourself."

"Is this a gender thing?"

"See? I knew you'd say that. I see it as more of a you have

no experience with winter weather conditions here and you don't have anyone to back you up when something goes wrong *thing*. Call it a safety concern." His gaze raked over her leaving fire in its wake. "Where are you from?"

"Manhattan."

He muttered something suspiciously like, "Dear God," and his eyes met hers.

"Something wrong with Manhattan?" she asked.

"Do you know anything about living on a ranch? Anything at all?"

She so badly wanted to say yes, but the honest answer was, "No. But I am here to learn."

LORD SAVE HIM from rich city girls. Seth gave her a week. Less than a week and she'd be gone. Which should have made him happy but all he felt was a deep and unwavering unease at the thought of her out here by herself. "You do realize this place has sat empty for years. Do you even know if your heating works?"

"Not yet. But the electricity's on, so it's a start and I guess I'll find out soon enough."

She sounded so proud of herself, but all he could do was close his eyes and try not to groan. He didn't need a clueless heiress on his doorstep. He didn't want a helpless waif to have to rescue, even if she was the most beautiful waif he'd ever seen. "Lady—"

"Maddie or Madeline, please. And never call me Love. I know it's my surname but just… don't."

If he'd grown up with Love as his surname, he'd probably feel the same way. "Look… Maddie—"

She nodded as if he'd pleased her and he ground his teeth in irritation, because it hadn't been a hardship to call her by her name. A big, huge hunk of him that resided below his waist just plain liked the way her name sounded on his lips.

"Your electricity company won't come unless they have access to the place and seeing as I had to plow my way in here this morning, all two miles of your private gravel road, starting from the turnoff to *my* family's ranch, my guess is they haven't been by. Your electricity's not on."

"Oh."

"And if you don't have electricity on out here you will freeze." Just in case she didn't quite understand.

"But they can come in now, can't they? Now that you've plowed?"

"Yes, and they'll come, and you'll stay and then you won't be able to drive your way out." And he'd worry about her. He didn't want to worry about her and take to calling in on her every other day and being her good-guy white knight. Been there done that with another woman long ago and didn't care to repeat the experience, thank you, no.

She shoved her hands in her coat pockets and ducked her

head and scuffed at the snow he'd tramped down already. "Right. So, I need to call the electricity people again and let them know the way is clear and then I need to find someone who'll come out and plow my road as often as need be. No problem. I can do that." But her voice had grown more uncertain, and he was acutely aware she had no knowledge of this valley or the people in it.

She took a breath and lifted her chin and her beauty hit him square in the gut all over again. It was her eyes. He'd never seen eyes so expressive. Golden-eagle-colored, thickly fringed eyes set wide apart in a face that could grace any billboard.

And sure, she seemed dressed for warmth apart from her lack of gloves, so she hadn't rocked up entirely unprepared. She drove a top-of-the-range 4WD—a safe choice for winter conditions. And there was no better way to get a feel for how inhospitable winter living in the valley could be than to experience it. But her ranch house was huge and had been neglected for way too many years. Her heat pump would need work. Her water pipes would need filling and flushing, assuming they hadn't frozen, burst, and subsequently been leaking for years. There could be critters in the house, although he hadn't seen any tracks in the snow around the broken window. She needed to source and chop wood if she didn't have any stored. She'd be shoveling snow for hours just to clear a path from the house to the garage. The list went on and on.

Even *he* wouldn't be up for resurrecting this place on his own.

"Okay, Maddie, I'm going to do you one favor and one favor only, so don't go expecting more."

She looked at the boarded-up window. "Haven't you already done it?"

But he'd already fished out his phone, no point stopping now. "Hey, Jill, it's Seth. I hear you have a crew scheduled to power up the Love ranch in Serenity Valley? Yeah, that's right, the way's clear. It's one of mine now." He nodded, presumably listening to what Jill had to say. "Appreciate it."

"One of yours?" Madeline asked when he ended the call and there was a lilt in her voice that wasn't charming, nope, no siree, not at all.

"They'll do it faster if they think I'm working out here. As for you getting snowed in, there's a young guy, Brody, who lives about five miles north along the highway. I'll have work for him come summer, but I don't have anything for him now. He's close enough to know the weather and can plow your access road when he does his own. I know he won't say no to the work. You want me to line him up to come by and discuss terms?"

"That's three favors—"

"No one likes a smart-ass, Maddie. This isn't a favor for you—it's for Brody."

"Oh, I see. My mistake. By all means do that favor for Brody."

Man, could her eyes glow when she was smiling.

"I'd love to get him on board for some snowplowing." She looked around. "And probably other stuff. What do you think he'd be like at maintenance and repair?"

"Not nearly good enough." If she thought he was going to let anyone but a professional touch this house, she was sadly mistaken.

"I don't suppose *you'd* be interested in doing any renovation work that needs doing?" She gestured awkwardly toward the sign on the side of his truck. "By that, I mean I would employ your company to do the work."

"I'm scheduled out for the next eighteen months."

"You must be good."

"So they say." He'd worked hard to become so. "Apart from that, I've wanted to get my hands on this house since I was old enough to swing a hammer. If your renovation plans don't mesh with mine, I'd fight like the devil to change your way of thinking. That what you want?"

"That's the last thing I want, no offense. I know what I'm doing. I'm an interior designer and this is about to become my showpiece."

Was that supposed to fill him with confidence? She probably had six different favorite white paint colors and an obsession with *feel* and *flow*. Mood boards would be a thing. Practicality would vanish, no match for artistic vision. He'd worked with interior designers before.

"Did you just groan?" she asked.

"Maybe."

"I… see."

Probably best if she didn't. "You want to park your car in the garage?" The barn was closer, but the garage would likely have more heating options.

"I—guess the garage? Although it's a long way from the house so maybe I could park in the barn instead?"

And that right there was the problem. Interior designer Madeline from Manhattan didn't know what she didn't know.

He collected his tools and started making his way back to the truck. "I'm going to clear your way to the garage and then I'm going to give you my business card and be on my way." He couldn't stay and help her out. He'd be here all day. "Once you've had a good look around, I sincerely hope you're going to drive to Marietta and book into a B&B for a few nights. If you want to go upscale, stay at the Graff Hotel."

"Are you telling me what to do?"

"No, because I used the words sincerely and hope. This is what I hope you'll do. Once you've settled in and asked anyone at all who's the best builder around these parts, I recommend you call me and say, 'Seth, I've had a look around and bringing my ranch house out of a fourteen yearlong shutdown is beyond me. I will pay you handsomely for your trouble if you'll bring your electricians, plumbers, and heating specialists in to get my place up and running safely. At which point I'm going to say, good idea, *Maddie*. Give me four days and I'll get it done."

"You said you were booked out for eighteen months."

"I'll make the time."

"So, you'll be doing this as a favor. For me."

"Absolutely not." He loaded his truck and got in the driver's seat, trying to figure his way out of this one. "Couple of my crew could use a bit of overtime. Don't worry—I'll be charging like a wounded bull and passing the money through to them."

"So you're doing *them* a favor?"

"Exactly." Was she really buying his bullshit? "You only get one favor, Maddie. No exceptions." He fished around in his glovebox for a business card and handed it to her.

"If I were to say thank you, would that imply that I think you're doing me a favor, or could we just write it off as a simple case of good manners?"

There were those smiley eyes again, joined by plump and perfect lips lifting, parting to reveal even white teeth and… dimples.

Given everything else she had going for her, dimples were downright unfair. "Keep an eye on the sky," he muttered gruffly. "There's more snow forecast later this afternoon and it'll take you at least half an hour to get to Marietta from here."

"Nice to meet you," she offered politely as he started the engine.

"If you're ever looking to sell," he began, "now would be a really good time."

She crossed her arms defensively in front of her and took a step back. "I'll keep that in mind."

He cleared the way to the garage for her and manually opened the doors once she'd found the right set of keys to open the padlock. She waved as he drove away and he lifted his hand in reply, same as he'd do for anyone.

She wasn't special. He wasn't worried about leaving her all alone out here, no sir.

But he watched her in his rearview mirror as she fished a shovel from the back of her car and started walking toward the front door. Watched until the driveway curved and he couldn't see her anymore.

He could've shoveled a path to her front door in ten... fifteen minutes flat.

But that would have been doing her a favor.

Chapter Four

IT TOOK MADELINE over an hour to clear a path from the garage to the front portico and another ten minutes after that to clear the snow off the steps and away from the huge double entrance doors. She should have bought her daypack and a bottle of water with her on the trek, she should probably walk back to the car and get it, following the path she'd just created. Hydration was important after exercise.

But she just plain didn't have the energy to walk back for water and then shuffle her way back to the front doors again. Better to use that energy to put her shoulder to the doors she'd just unlocked and *push*.

The doors opened with a groan and a waft of cold, dank air washed over her and made her shudder.

Welcome home, Maddie. Where've you been all this time?

The entrance alcove was darker than she remembered, the central atrium still awe inspiring. She walked the perimeter of the main room, pushing dusty blue velvet curtains aside to let in some light. The rest of the ground floor consisted of a residential wing.

Her feet took her past the door to her parents' bedroom

suite, past her grandmother's bedroom door, and on to the sunroom at the end of the corridor, her heart pounding and her vision blurring as old memories broke free to mingle among the staleness and decay of a house that hadn't felt footsteps in years.

She put her hand to the doorknob and closed her eyes. If her memories held true, this room, more than any other, would tell her whether her father had simply closed the door on this house after her mother's death and never returned.

Deep breath, Madeline. You've got this.

The room was steeped in sunlight, no dusty velvet curtains for these enormous windows. An empty hospital bed stood near the window, still tilted so that a person who could no longer sit up on their own could look out the window and see nothing but sky and mountains in the distance.

To her everlasting relief, the bed had been stripped and a set of sheets and coverlet sat neatly folded, maybe even laundered, on the end of the bed.

She lurched forward on suddenly wooden legs as she spotted the jigsaw puzzle on the round table in the corner. *Blink.* She was back in this room at eleven years old sitting quietly as Marta, the day nurse, fussed with fresh flowers in the vase by the window and checked her dozing mother's pulse with a touch. *Blink.* Back to today with no vase in sight but the unfinished puzzle still firmly in place.

Blink.

Her father hadn't been there at the very end when they'd

needed him the most. She'd fought with him as he'd walked out the door to the waiting helicopter. Thrown a tantrum. Wept. *Daddy, stay. Why won't you stay?* What kind of father left an eleven-year-old alone with her dying mother and one palliative care nurse who was only supposed to be there during the day?

Blink. Her father had been gone three days when her mother shook her head and pushed the chicken broth aside and asked Marta if she could stay the night, please, and Marta had agreed.

Marta hadn't made Madeline go to sleep in her own room that night. Instead, they'd collected up Madeline's blankets and pillows and brought them to the sunshine room and together they'd made a nest on the sofa and filled the little side table next to it with books and toys and a little music player.

Blink. The sofa nest and toys were gone but the little pink cassette player remained.

Sniff. Let the memories come—just get them out of the way. Madeline had woken before the dawn, and Marta had smiled from her own nest of pillows and blankets on the window seat and told Madeline to take her mother's hand and describe the sunrise.

Her mother had passed as faint light stole across the valley and only then had Madeline let go and cried.

Marta had said it was as peaceful a passing as any she'd seen, and then held Madeline in her arms and together they'd recited the Lord's Prayer and watched the day unfold.

Blink. Nothing but blue sky and mountain views in Madeline's world now. One of these days, she vowed, she was going to claim back sunrises as the start of a wonderful new day rather than a witness to the kindness of strangers and unspeakable sorrow.

Marta had tidied this room before leaving. Madeline knew it the way she knew her own name. She trailed her fingertips over the utilitarian hospital bed and sat on the window seat, her back propped against the wall as Marta's had been.

She pulled her knees up to her chest and wrapped her arms around her legs and rested her head against her knees and felt young and helpless and lost all over again.

This house, this valley in all its snowbound beauty was hers now, handed down from one generation of women to the next. A home once so full of love Madeline could barely stand to remember it.

She closed her eyes and prayed for the strength to fill it with love again.

Chapter Five

I N ALL HIS many calculations, when it came to acquiring the Love ranch, Seth had never once factored in Jonas Love's daughter. Oh, he'd figured she might inherit it when her father died—at which point she'd gratefully offload it to him—but never once had he considered that the ranch already belonged to her, had been held in trust for her, just waiting for her to reach a certain age and claim it.

How old was she anyway? She had a way of answering questions as if she was asking for permission. Twenty-one? Not that young. Twenty-five? That seemed about right. Not thirty. He was over thirty, no need to remind him, and there was still no sign of his dream wife and family.

Not that he was waiting... more that he was open to the notion. He knew what he wanted and when he found it, he would act.

His future wife would not be flaky. No moonlit yoga bubbles for her. She wouldn't be city bred either, forever longing for a lifestyle he couldn't give her. She'd know the value of family and hard work, and she'd look up when he walked into a room and her golden eyes would light up at the sight of him and—*hold up*.

Since when had his fantasy wife acquired smiling golden eyes, auburn hair, warm hands and a strong desire to never ever be called love?

He'd waited all last night for her call. Even left his phone on his bedstand, something he never did, but she hadn't called.

She hadn't called this morning either and it was now going on for lunch break and he refused to pull his phone out and check for messages yet again.

He was working, dammit!

His brother Jett—who often swung a hammer for him when he wasn't skiing—had been eyeing him strangely all morning, finally spoke up. "What's eating you?"

"Not a damn thing. You finished that section yet? Not paying you to stand around gasbagging."

"You're not paying me at all, pardner." Jett none too subtly reminded him that Seth wasn't the only one with a financial stake in the business. It wasn't fifty-fifty, but Jett's startup money had bankrolled the company in the early days and Seth meticulously paid his brother a percentage of the company profits. But, yeah, his brother didn't pull a daily wage when he did put in some hours. It wasn't about the money—Jett had said as much the rare times Seth had brought it up.

Maybe it was time to check in on that again. "If you want a wage, say so."

Jett studied him with a frown Seth sometimes saw when looking in a mirror. Stubborn chin, lips pressed thin, determined glint in his eyes. "I repeat, what's eating you that has half your crew threatening to walk off the job if someone doesn't take you aside and hose you down? Guess who got voted in?"

"I haven't been that bad."

The cynical arch of his brother's raised eyebrow suggested otherwise.

Okay, maybe he had been riding his crew harder than usual this morning, but only because he was about to pull half of them off the job once a pretty Manhattan socialite gave him the nod. "I met Madeline Love yesterday. She told me the ranch doesn't belong to her father at all, he was just the trustee or guardian or whatever you want to call it until she came of age."

Jett didn't seem surprised. "Mardie worked the bar at the Graff last night. Your little heiress was asking about you."

"She's not that little." And she sure as hell wasn't his.

"Mardie liked her."

Jett's wife hadn't always been a good judge of character in her early years—some lessons had to be learned the hard way—but Seth trusted Mardie's take on people these days. She'd married his brother, after all. "I offered to get the Love ranch up and running for her. Told her to give me a call."

"And?"

Wasn't it obvious? "She hasn't called."

"Her loss, brother."

And then his phone rang. Seth didn't recognize the number, and it shocked him just how much he wanted it to be Madeline Love calling him no matter what the reason.

"'Lo." He sounded surly and knew it, and his mood didn't improve when his brother snorted and walked away. Seth wasn't acting all out of character on account of a woman.

He was all out of sorts because he wanted her *house*.

"Seth, it's Madeline Love. I'm calling from the Graff. Good idea, by the way. Do you want to have yesterday's conversation all over again or can I just say that I want to employ you and your crew to bring my house out of hibernation?"

"You can just say that."

"What kind of exorbitant price are we looking at?"

"Won't know 'til I've had a look." He wouldn't overcharge her, but she didn't have to know that. He had to save face somehow.

"What are you doing this afternoon?"

"You just want me for my snowplow." Was he *flirting* with her now? Because it seemed a whole lot like he was. He ran a hand through his hair and started pacing, well aware of the looks he was getting from his crew. Seth Casey did not get flustered by a woman. He had plenty of moves when it came to women, and they were all smooth.

"Brody's out there doing that now. I don't want to hold

anyone up when it comes to getting started. I'm after a cleaning crew too. I want the inside scoured from top to bottom. And painters. I'm going to need painters too."

"Let me guess—you want Benjamin Moore, Antique White from top to bottom."

"Wash your mouth out." Was she laughing at him or herself? "Antique White is so yesterday."

"So, are you doing it up to sell or are you planning to stick around after the new year?"

"I'm staying." She sounded quietly sure about that decision. "I'm going to make the ranch my home. Maybe not year-round, maybe not the cattle raising part, but the home won't sit empty for another fourteen years. You have my word."

Hopefully, she was fickle and flighty. Born and bred with big city lights in mind. "Not much call for interior designers around here."

"If I get it right, clients from all over the world will come to me."

"Big call."

"I'm tired of being the most unimportant person in the room. I'm sick of my goals and needs not being seen and I aim to change that. There. You're the first person I've ever said that to."

"Maddie." He was a terrible father confessor. "At least put a drink in front of a man and warn him before you get all... deep. Give him a chance to run."

"You are so sweet."

"Now you're just insulting me. Seth Casey is a hard-ass. He is not and never will be sweet. Ask anyone."

"Oh, I have. Your sister-in-law was working the bar here last night. She thinks you're a handyman legend, great with kids, and a total sweetheart. The best of what's left of the unattached Casey men."

"The—she said that?"

"She, of course, got the very best of the Casey men, but I figure she's obliged to say that whether it's true or not. Oh, and before you go, can you point me in the direction of your favorite local kitchen manufacturer? I'm going shopping."

"What's wrong with your current kitchen?"

"Have you *seen* it?"

No, no he hadn't. "Let me take a look before you do anything rash."

"Seth, sweetheart, back off."

And if that didn't bring the stubborn bull out in him he didn't know what would. "My crew will be at the house at nine thirty in the morning." And so would he. "Someone needs to be there to let us in."

"I'll be there. I found a spare set of keys in the terrible, horrible, no good, very bad kitchen. I'll give them to you then."

SETH CASEY WAS back in her space and looking even finer than he had two days ago. Madeline watched from her freshly cleared front steps as he closed the door on his truck, squared his shoulders, and headed her way with long, lean strides that covered a whole lot of ground in a very short time. One side of his lips hiked up in what she badly wanted to look on as a smile, and she smiled back, determined to present a picture of sunshine and light, no bone-deep uncertainty about her future on show. She was Madeline Love, future interior designer to the stars, newest member of the Serenity Valley community and, give or take a hospital bed full of memories, happy to be here.

Amazing what a great steak dinner and a night at a five-star gorgeously appointed historical hotel could do. Her *Hi, I'm Madeline Love from the Love ranch in Serenity Valley. Seth Casey suggested I hit you up for a room for a night or two*, had brought open doors, warm welcome, an upgraded room, and a free drink at the bar where she'd met Mardie Casey, who'd laughed long and loud when Madeline recounted Seth's problem when it came to doing her any favors.

"He wants that place so bad," Mardie had said between grins. "He always has."

"But why?" she'd asked. "Is it the location?"

"That and a lot of respect for the craftsmen who built it. There aren't many old homes like that around here and they're tightly held. He'll be disappointed you're not looking to sell. He'll still help you though, if he said he would. He's a man of his word."

Madeline had stayed at the bar and ordered another drink, just so she could hear Seth's sister-in-law tell tall tales about all those Casey boys. She felt like she knew him just that little bit better because of it.

"Beautiful day," she said, as he drew closer. The sky was blue, the air was brisk. Her fingers hadn't yet frozen stiff.

"That it is."

He wore a cowboy hat today, black as his eyes, and he took it off as they stepped inside. She'd chocked the double doors open, figuring tradesmen would be coming in and out and he frowned at that but made no comment.

"How long since you've seen inside the house?" she asked.

"Years. But I remember coming here as a kid."

"Funny." She didn't remember ever meeting him *or* any of his brothers. "Did my family and yours have a falling out? It's just, I don't remember meeting any of you when I was a kid."

"Safe to say we ran in different social circles," he said. "And I'm likely a dozen years older than you are."

"How old are you?" It was a rude question, but he'd left that door wide open, hadn't he?

"Thirty-three."

"Eight years older than me."

He studied her face, a long, slow look that added heat to her cheeks and a flutter to her pulse before he finally turned away. She should have taken that as her cue to stop staring at him, but she became captivated by the unfiltered delight on his face as he entered the main living room with the soaring atrium and stone wall features. His happiness softened the rough-cut edges of his face and dialed back his commanding presence, making her want to keep right on watching him enjoy the space he now occupied.

"Hello, beautiful," he murmured, looking up. "You crazy, gorgeous place."

No denying that.

Take one rustic Montana mountain theme and dial it up to a thousand, and it still wouldn't prepare a person for the overwhelming amount of timber, stone, and ironwork the place contained. Cascading chandeliers hung from the high-vaulted ceiling and looking up toward the first floor that framed that soaring space, you could see walkway railings and a hint of the many bookshelves and doorways beyond. Apart from two reading alcoves, that first floor housed another six bedrooms and an office. The lower ground floor contained a long bar, mudrooms and showers geared toward skiers or lumberjacks. The ground level held a large living area, formal and informal dining rooms, kitchen, and the main bedroom suite and guest bedroom suite.

There were windows in the main living room, but they weren't overly large, and she'd always wondered why not. There were other design choices she wouldn't have made had she been building from scratch. Why sink a lounge in the middle of a room so that no one sitting there could look at anything but a wall of rock and a fireplace capable of roasting a whole beast at a time? Why add *more* wooden furniture to the mix, as if they weren't already surrounded by enough timber to fill a lumberyard?

They made their way farther into the main room, Seth looking like a man in love.

With her house...

"So, above all, this is a masculine space and I'm guessing that's why you like it so much," she mused aloud. "You can see yourself and your family here with you, filling it up with your big bold selves and life and laughter and the next generation of Montana cowboys and craftsmen. You fit."

"Well, yeah. There's that. Are you saying you don't fit in here? Because from where I'm standing you don't look that out of place."

"Compliments will get you dazzling smiles and more confessions from me. Brace yourself."

He gave her a long-suffering look that made her unaccountably happy.

"My father and his new family are joining me here for Christmas this year. He's moved on, and I need to show him that I can move on too and be a part of his new world and not be left out and stuck in the past. So I want new paint and a new kitchen, picture windows all the way along that wall and I'm in two minds about putting new flooring straight across the sunken lounge area."

"And you want it done when?"

"By Christmas."

"Paint, yes. Kitchen maybe. You won't get custom-made windows before Christmas and as for making the sunken lounge area disappear..." He headed for the sunken lounge area and stared down into the pit at the circular lounge and coffee table. "What's wrong with it?"

"Try it."

She stayed where she was, leaning over the railing as he descended and made himself at home, legs wide, head back and arms out as he stared up at the first-floor landing and then the ceiling. His smile bloomed and it was breathtaking.

"Reckon your family would all fit?"

"Hell, yes."

She reached for the hidden button and pressed it, praying the mechanism still worked, and watched Seth's reaction as a circular wooden slab rose from the center of the coffee table to allow a small circular drinks bar to rise from center of the table, the round cushion in the very center of the circle. From memory, the little bar had four sections: two containing glassware, one with an ice bucket, and the last with a couple of bottles of bourbon.

He looked. Looked closer. "Sweet Mother of—"

"Yep. I'm pretty sure you can blame my mother's mother for everything down there. What can I say? It was the seventies."

"But, Maddie. How old's the bourbon?"

So much for the revolutionary interior design. "Does it say on the bottle?"

"PAPPY VAN WINKLE. EIGHTEEN-YEAR-OLD SPECIAL RESERVE FAMILY SELECTION made in—" He choked on whatever he'd been aiming to say. "Maddie, I'm sorry but I'm never coming out." He looked to where the walls of the sunken lounge area met the regular floor level and his eyes narrowed as if in consideration. "Why would you want to get rid of this? It's cozy. Unique."

"Can you put a wooden floor over it?"

"Yes, but—"

"*Psst.*"

He stopped. "What is *psst* in New York terms?"

"It means stop talking."

But clearly he disagreed because he started right back up again, messing with her vision. "I could do a parquetry floor in the round that could come and go at will, give or take a couple of strong guys who could put it together and take it apart. That way you'd get the best of both worlds. A ballroom area or whatever the hell kind of flat floor area you're thinking of when you're looking to entertain the masses, and this cozy family area when you're not.

Seth Casey had quite the imagination. And that was before he started in on the bourbon. "Have you ever done a floor like that before?"

"For this house, I would make an exception."

As opposed to making an exception for *her*. She snorted

softly at his continued inability to acknowledge that, yes, he was doing her many favors, but she didn't call him on it. "Is that a no to having any experience with temporary floating floors? I'm thinking that's a no you haven't and mine would be the guinea pig."

"This other bottle's a TWENTY-THREE-YEAR-OLD FAMILY RESERVE. Unopened," he said. "It could probably pay for the floor."

"You do realize there's a perfectly good wet bar downstairs, full of stuff like that?" *Oh. My. How to make a man whimper.* "You don't have a drinking problem, do you?"

"Not yet."

"Because this place would be a bad purchase for anyone wanting to stay dry, what with this and the bar downstairs and the taproom and the wine cellar and all."

"Now you're just trying to make me cry."

"Can I show you the kitchen next?" Because, seriously. There was only so much of a reclining, blissed-out Seth Casey that she could stand to see at one time.

The kitchen was dated, very dated and there wasn't much to love.

Seth, on the other hand, seemed wholly in love with the wood-fire oven and heating system and the big old ceramic tubs better suited to a laundry or washing potatoes for a hundred people. Up close, the stone wall and fireplace shared by the living room could probably spit roast an entire cow while also doubling as a rock-climbing wall for the intrepid guest. First to the top got to hang their hat on the antlers up there.

"I've never seen this fireplace in use. Not once," she said. "All it does is draw cold air down and in."

Moments later the top half of him had disappeared up inside the chimney, leaving her to stare at the parts of him that remained in view. How could she not stare at such strong, solid thighs and spectacularly ample... centerpiece? Because the fabric of his jeans looked old and stretched and outlined every lovely line. "Are you left-handed?"

"Yep."

Because he absolutely and unequivocally dressed to the left.

He said something else, but she was too busy putting her hands to her cheeks to try and control her blush to hear what he said. It wasn't until he bent down and caught her staring that she stammered a hasty, "Sorry, what was that?"

"Why did you ask if I was left-handed?"

"Just a wild guess."

"Uh-huh."

His deliciously slow drawl didn't help her blushing problem at all.

But his top half disappeared up the chimney again. "Can you see an iron ring pull on either side, about halfway up? Pull on the rings and you'll lift a pair of steel plates into place. They're a feature of these types of fireplace."

"I didn't know that."

"Wouldn't have mattered if you had. They're stuck. I'd like to fix that and season the ironwork. No charge—just pure appreciation for old-fashioned craftwork. That okay by you?"

"Sure. Put it on my tab."

"How attached to your clothes are you?"

Madeline felt her eyes widen, and truly didn't know how to answer him. She had a feeling she'd be replaying this scene over and over and dreaming up ever more unlikely responses. She huffed a laugh, and he had the grace to look ever so slightly embarrassed.

"I find them fairly useful," she finally managed.

He cleared his throat. "I wondered if you wanted to step in and take a look, that's all, but it's sooty and there's no need." He eased out of the space and landed lightly on his feet for such a big man.

"You just geeked out over a chimney fitting." Was he *blushing*?

"Guilty."

She *liked* this man. "You really do like this place, don't you?"

"I've wanted it for as long as I can remember. Look at it."

And now he was making *her* feel guilty. "Why are you being so nice to me when it would be in your best interest to see that I have a terrible stay here and never want to return?"

"Don't be insulting."

"I—" Had she insulted him? From the stern set of his jaw it seemed she had. "Apologize?"

"Maybe it *is* that cutthroat where you come from but that's not me. People before possessions, Maddie. Understand?"

"I—yes?" It wasn't that hard a concept to understand. "I understand."

"Where'd you learn to expect the worst from people?" he asked, and she shrugged rather than confess the role her father had played in her world view of putting most everything and everyone else before her.

"I... don't know."

"Yeah, you do." He stared at the rest of the old kitchen for a very long time. He seemed to be weighing her words or maybe figuring his next move. "Maybe you need to expect more of people," he said and there was a gentleness about those quietly spoken words that pierced what little armor she had left against him.

"I—yes. Good idea." She needed to get away from him and rebuild her defenses. "I'll be cataloging furniture this morning, starting with the treasure trove in the basement. If anyone needs me, that's where I'll be. I bought bottled water for everyone. It's on the kitchen counter. I didn't know if the water in the pipes was going to be any good straight away, so..."

"Appreciate that. I'll be here to set everyone up and then I'll be heading off to another job and I'll be back at the end of the day."

She nodded and turned to leave, and then backtracked in order to take a water bottle for herself. "Thank you for helping me make this place habitable again. Thank you for keeping me safe."

"Don't mention it."

"Why, because then you'd have to acknowledge that you're doing me many favors?" She turned and headed for the basement stairs, mainly because his shocked confusion was just too cute to bear. "You're a strange, sweet man, Seth Casey," she said, a little louder so he could hear her.

"I mean it," he warned, and he could speak louder too. "Don't mention it!"

Glee was a wonderful emotion, Madeline decided as she kept right on walking. She needed more of it in her world.

Chapter Six

"HEY, MOM." SETH left his boots in the mudroom and hung his coat on his peg before stepping into his mother's kitchen, too well trained to do otherwise. She'd raised five boys and had no time at all for unnecessary housework. He'd railed against her house rules as a kid but as an adult he thanked her for teaching him to respect and care for what was his and pay the same respect for what belonged to others.

His mother looked up from the jigsaw puzzle spread out on the kitchen table. "I wasn't expecting you today. I've been trying to clean out the attic and get your brothers to either collect all their teenage trophies and schoolbooks or let me toss them, but do you think I can get them to cooperate?" She placed a jigsaw piece in the correct spot with a satisfied nod. "You'd think I was erasing their existence."

"You haven't asked me to come and get all my stuff yet."

"That's because all your stuff is in the basement and I haven't finished in the attic yet."

Made sense. "So who owns the jigsaw puzzle?" He vaguely remembered working on it when he was a kid, one time when they were snowed in. All one thousand five hundred pieces of arctic wolf against a snowy mountain background. There'd been one damn piece missing when they'd finished, and he debated whether to tell his mother that now but decided against it.

Maybe it had magically reappeared.

"I think you might own this puzzle? Do you want it?"

"No." He backed away fast and then added a quick "thank you" instead of a hell no. "I don't have time for that. Can I grab a coffee and pick your brain?"

"What do you want to know?"

"I've just been up at the Love ranch talking to Madeline Love. Did you know she owned the place and not her father? And now she's old enough to claim it and claim it she has. She says she'll be here until the new year."

"Does she want to sell?"

"Probably not, but I'm not ruling out the thought that she won't like it here and that she will decide to move on and part with the place. What can you tell me about her?" He took two coffee mugs from the cupboard while he waited for her reply. It wouldn't do to appear too interested. His mother had two of her five sons married. Seth wasn't one of them.

His mother continued to scour the puzzle pieces for details only she knew. "I remember she was a pretty little baby with a wisp of red hair, big anxious eyes, and nature as shy as a fawn," she said with a fondness she usually reserved for soggy kittens.

"She's bigger these days."

"What's she like?" His mother neatly turned the question right back on him.

"Kind of—" Fragile, he wanted to say. Maybe even mistreated, although that was harder to say because she gave off such confusing signals. "It'd be easy to steamroll her," he said instead. "So I'm trying not to unless I think I'm right." Problem was, he was always right. "What else can you tell me about the family?"

"I know that Elise—Madeline's mother—married for love rather than money and that her fancy New York banker husband doted on her and on Madeline too. I know that Elise's mother Peggy—she was the one who bought the ranch in the first place—died in a boating accident and that Elise passed away not too many months later. It was like a double family tragedy. Just gutted the heart of the family."

"How did Madeline's mother die?"

"Lymphoma. She died up at the ranch. I know young Madeline was up there 'til the very end. I'm not sure the husband was."

"How do I not know any of this?" Dying neighbors didn't go unnoticed around here.

"You'd have been around nineteen or twenty. Might have happened when you were up in Kalispell apprenticing for that carpenter."

Ah. Sounded about right.

His mother looked up from the puzzle to meet his gaze. "The only other news I've ever heard was that young Madeline ended up in boarding school in Upstate New York and her father went back to work on Wall Street and turned a small fortune into a large one. Did you ask her what she does for a living?"

"She's an interior designer."

He came by his smirk honestly. His mother had one just like it and she was wearing it now because she'd heard him curse far too many interior designers to the depths of hell as he and his crew attempted to *realize their vision*. He set a mug of coffee, heavy on the creamer, down in front of her just as his oldest brother stomped in.

"Any more coffee on offer?" Mason asked. Silently, Seth returned to the counter and reached for another mug.

"Boots off," he said, just to rile the man.

Mason scowled but he retraced his steps and left his boots at the mudroom door. "Thought you'd be working."

Seth could've said the same, especially given the way Mason was dressed in a suit most ranchers would've reserved for christenings and funerals. Instead, he kept his thoughts to himself in an effort not to upset their mother. More and more since their father's death, Mason had been claiming the right to run the family ranch. It escaped no one's notice that his version of running the place didn't extend to doing much of the actual grunt work. "Just on my way back from the Love ranch."

His oldest brother's eyes narrowed. It was no secret that Mason had visions of acquiring the Love ranch and expanding Casey cattle growing operations, but he didn't have the money to do it. Seth, on the other hand, did have the money to buy the place outright and boy did that stick in his big brother's craw.

"Don't know why you want the place so bad," Mason muttered. "Not as if you'd put cattle on it and use it as it's meant to be used."

"Says who?" Seth leaned back against the counter and took a slow sip of his drink in an effort to curb his temper. He and his two younger brothers had recognized early on in life that the family ranch wouldn't keep five men employed. They'd each struck out on different paths and been successful. Whereas his two older brothers were still duking it out for control of the ranch. "Who are you to tell me what I would and wouldn't do? I've just as much ranching in my blood as you."

"Cut it out." His mother's word was law around here and Seth swallowed his anger along with another sip of coffee. "Seth was just saying young Madeline Love is up there at the moment."

Mason glanced Seth's way. "Is she blonde, helpless, and ready to screw you over—just the way you like them?"

That was the thing about family. Everyone knew where the bodies were buried. "Why are you harping on a relationship I put behind me years ago? At least I had a go, learned a thing or two, and moved on. I'm not the one standing around all proud and bitter and still stuck on a woman who left me for dust years ago. That would be you."

"Boys!"

The word cracked like a whip as Seth set his barely touched coffee on the counter, crossed to his mother and gave her a brief farewell kiss. "Gotta get to work anyway."

The last glance Seth had was of Mason picking up Seth's abandoned coffee and settling into the space Seth had abandoned.

I'll take what's yours, buddy. Mason's actions couldn't have spoken any clearer. *I'll make myself right at home.*

Fucking firstborns.

Chapter Seven

THREE DAYS LATER, Madeline moved in, forever grateful to the tradespeople and cleaners who'd worked alongside her and made the place gleam. She'd cataloged the contents and had never before had such a treasure trove of furniture and artwork to work with. She'd found filing cabinets stuffed full of purchase history and provenance for so many of the pieces along with her grandmother Peggy's handwritten thoughts for where they might go. She hadn't even *known* of her grandmother's passion for fine furnishings, and it made her so happy to have that connection to the past.

She'd taken to sending Bette pictures of her favorite finds and then waiting for Bette to phone her, just so she could hear Bette's telling her in her New York accent that Madeline was killing her, and to keep the pictures coming because her customers were getting used to seeing her drool.

Bette missed her and wasn't shy about saying so. Madeline missed Bette too. Her midmorning coffee just wasn't the same without Bette's caustic commentary about clients who knew what they wanted but didn't quite understand why they couldn't have it given their current constraints.

Madeline too had current constraints but now that everyone had gone, today was the day she tackled the contents of the main bedroom. Her bedroom now, should she choose to accept that particular challenge, but first she had to empty it.

Maybe this was what her father had been talking about when he'd said he wanted all trace of her mother gone. Maybe all he really wanted was not to have to deal with closets full of his late wife's clothes.

In a fit of foresight, she'd collected packing boxes and tape and lined them up along the bedroom wall, ready for filling. The problem being that in the three hours she'd been at it, all she'd managed to do was fill a couple of boxes with her father's old clothes and shoes. He wouldn't want them—he'd left nothing of any significant monetary value, but she'd left a message with Symonds just in case.

As far as boxing up her mother's clothes were concerned, she'd stalled the moment she'd opened the top drawer of the walnut dresser. A waft of sweet orange and geranium perfume had assaulted her senses and she'd hightailed it out to the kitchen and made herself a cup of willow tea with shaking hands.

Her mother had worn brightly colored scarves to cover her baldness in those last few months of life. That drawer was full of scarves.

No wonder her father wanted them gone. Some memories were simply too hard to hold.

So get with the program, Madeline, and pack up the scarves.

Cancer was a brutal illness as so many people knew. Plenty of other daughters had been tasked with sorting through their dead mother's belongings. She wasn't alone.

C'mon, Maddie. You've got this. You can do this.

It's time.

She was back in the bedroom, packing the scarves into a box when the front doorbell rang. That she headed for the door as fast as her feet could take her was a measure of how heavy she found her packing task, no matter the pep talks she'd taken to voicing out loud.

The woman standing at the door and wearing an old blue beanie and an olive-green coat had a plate of food in her hand and lively green eyes.

Madeline had seen eyes that shape before, even if the color was different, and very recently too. "Hi! Welcome. Come in," she bubbled nervously.

"You don't even know me," said the woman.

"You're Seth's mom."

"Okay, mind reader, you're right. I come bearing brownies."

"You do?" It wasn't that she didn't like brownies. She loved sweets. It was the whole idea of someone's mother taking the time out of their day to bake something for her that didn't make sense. "Please, come in. And please, keep your boots on," she added as the other woman handed her the plate of brownies and bent to undo her laces.

"I brought inside shoes to put on," the older woman said. "They're in my bag and I'm happy to wear them as long as you don't mind me making myself at home. No point making more cleaning work for you. I'm sure you have better things to do. Which reminds me, let me know if you want me to put you in touch with a cleaner. Coralie May has a son who just finished school and is looking for work. He lives two ranches over and he'll do anything. I can vouch for him being a hard worker."

"Are you talking about Brody? Because Seth already put me onto him. He's down for plowing my drive and keeping me in wood."

"That's the one." The older woman slid her feet into a pair of flats shoes, straightening again to look at Madeline with kindly eyes. "I'm Savannah. You were a girl last time we met, and I doubt you remember me."

Madeline definitely didn't remember her. "Were you friends with my parents?"

"Friendly neighbors who socialized together every now and again, more like. I'm not looking to claim a relationship with them that I never had. I'm mainly here to let you know that you can call on me if ever you're in a bind. We take care of our own out here."

"But… I'm not a local."

"I think three generations of ownership of this place makes you more than a stranger. Don't you?"

She truly didn't know what to think about that. Mainly because, until a week or two ago, she hadn't known she owned the ranch at all. She'd let it go years ago and was only just becoming reacquainted with it. "Would you like a coffee to go with these brownies?"

"Sure. Seth said you're an interior designer."

"Yes." Madeline led the other woman into the kitchen. "Did he say it with that little tick he gets at the side of his mouth when something isn't to his liking?"

"Oh, you noticed that?" His mother laughed. "Not exactly subtle, that boy."

Not exactly a boy anymore either. Madeline and her chimney stack fantasies could vouch for that. Time to change the subject.

"You'd think giving this place a makeover would be easy for me, right? There's so much beauty here already. All the custom-made furniture that speaks to time and place and is old enough to be fashionable again," Madeline confessed.

She set the brownies on the counter and turned to find the older woman standing in the doorway, looking around with her hands in pockets of her winter jacket. "May I take your coat? I know it's still not as warm in here as it could be." She looked to the unlit fireplace, with the wood already in place just waiting for a match. Seth had set it for her, showing her how to do it, but it just seemed so wasteful to light it when she was the only one around.

Although she wasn't the only one here anymore.

"You want me to get that started?" asked Savannah, and Madeline nodded as she found some plates and napkins and took them to the breakfast nook. The bench seats and cozy informality of the little nook with its picture-window view to the north made it one of her favorite places in the house.

"I don't think anything's changed since I was here last," Savannah said once they'd made themselves comfortable and had hot drinks in hand.

"It probably hasn't. I'm cleaning out all my mother's stuff and it's time, I know it's time, but it's turning me into a wreck. I'm doing the bedroom and I opened a drawer of scarves just before you arrived and couldn't breathe for memories. Now it's all I can do to box up her clothes and push them into the hall, and even that…" She reached for a brownie. Brownies would definitely help. "I was hoping to get further than that. I was hoping to bin some of it and box some up for charity and just… get it done."

Savannah sat back, but her posture remained open as if to say *I'm listening, you're not scaring me off with your woe.*

But Madeline didn't have much more to add. "I'm struggling to stay on task."

"I know that feeling." Savannah nodded. "When my husband passed away, I was that person you just described. I wanted to say goodbye on my terms, and I didn't want my boys to see me break down so I sent them all away. I ended up setting one box aside, and in it I put items I knew he treasured. The watch his grandfather had given him. His wedding ring. His favorite shirt and his Sunday best. And then I filled it with the things *I* cherished that had belonged to him. The silly silk Christmas boxer shorts the boys had given him when they were kids. Some of the cards he wrote to me over the years. A sweater I'd knitted him that was the exact blue of his eyes. I kept the best of him, and then I sat there for what felt like a thousand years trying to figure out what to give the boys, because I didn't know if my heart could stand to see them wearing their father's clothes."

Madeline could only feel blessed by the other woman's openness. "What did you end up giving them?"

"Everything. Seth came in and caught me sobbing and soothed me with whiskey and asked if I trusted him enough to take everything that was left away and see to it that no one took too much or too little. He gave me a list of what they each took. Belts and buckles and hats, mainly. My three youngest each took a shirt. My oldest two took cuff links and quarreled over an expensive watch. Seth took the crappiest watch in the pack and asked me if I'd mind seeing it on a regular basis because he wanted to wear it to work. His father was so proud of him for striking out on his own and turning his mind to carpentry and building. What could I say but yes, wear the watch, your father would be so proud?"

"But… wasn't that insensitive of Seth? Doesn't it hurt you to see him wearing it?"

"Not anymore." Savannah Casey had such wise eyes. "I've come to understand that Seth needs that connection to his father. He doesn't get to live on the ranch and continue my husband's legacy the way my older boys do. He doesn't get to say this is where my father stood, and his father before him, and one day it's going to be mine. He has a shirt and a battered old watch and that's it. Who am I to deny him the simple wearing of a watch?"

"But… won't your sons share equally in any inheritance?"

"Not if they want to keep the ranch in the family. Jett's already relinquished his share—he's my youngest and he skis for a living, such a daredevil. I never knew half of what he and Tomas my second youngest got up to but if it was dangerous, they were sure to be in the thick of it. Tomas rode bucking bulls for years, but he's given that up now and is using his winnings to put himself through vet school. He's married now too, with a little boy. Then there's Seth, who has his own business and a couple of houses besides, but he's been saving to buy a ranch since he was seventeen and heaven only knows how much he's worth these days, but I do know he can afford to buy this place outright and still have change—that's if you've a mind to sell. And even if you don't and he ends up buying some other ranch around these parts, he'll be one for relinquishing his share in the family farm in exchange for some of our breeding stock. Those bloodlines are worth having. Which only leaves my two oldest battling it out for possession of the family ranch. No one's looking forward to that." The older woman seemed to age before Madeline's eyes. "Neither of them play fair."

Families were fascinating. This one made her head spin. Athletes. Bull riders. Builders. Ranchers. Inheritances. It almost made her grateful to be an only child.

Except that she wasn't an only child, not anymore.

And then another thought occurred to her. "Savannah, are you warning me away from your older sons?"

Savannah had a very rich and totally delicious brownie halfway to her mouth and Madeline's words stopped it in its tracks. The brownie went back on her plate as if suddenly tasteless. "I never thought of it that way."

It wasn't a no.

"What about Seth? Can I trust him?"

"You can trust him to the moon and back with your business. Same goes if you decide to sell to him—there's no one who'll take better care of this home."

Madeline nodded slowly, probably best not to ask for more. Wasn't as if she had designs on Savannah's middle son, because she didn't. He was just... sweet and strange. And helpful. She almost had him saying yes to helping her install a new kitchen before Christmas, even if he did steadfastly refuse to contemplate putting a bank of floor-to-ceiling feature windows in the main living room.

"As for Seth's heart... whoever claims that won't ever regret it. He knows how to give." Savannah *knew* what Madeline had been thinking. How could she know?

Savannah's laughter rang out, competing with the cheerful crackle and pop of the now merrily burning fire. "Seth's not the only one around here with a very expressive face."

"I don't have designs on him," Madeline protested weakly.

"But if you did, I wouldn't hold it against you," the other woman assured her, feeling around in her handbag and drawing out a business card. "Here's my number. Call me any time you like. You're welcome here, young Madeline. If you choose to make this your home and reach out to the people around you, you won't regret it."

"Thank you." Madeline rummaged in her handbag for a card to exchange as the other woman stood up, and then saw her to the door.

"Bring the plate back when you're done with it. It'll give you an excuse to call in."

Because apparently that was what neighbors did around here. "I can't promise a plate full of home-baked goods," Madeline warned. "I kind of don't cook. I'm hoping like hell I can get Christmas dinner catered."

Savannah laughed, a warm and cheerful sound. "Maybe someone in Marietta will help you with the prep so that all you'll have to do is put the turkey in the oven," she offered at last, still altogether too amused for comfort. "You look just like her, you know. Your mother."

"No, I don't. My mother was petite like a dancer. And beautiful. I'm neither."

"Look closer. And don't pack all her stuff away or get rid

of it in a rush. Find the pieces you cherish and then honor your memories of her by keeping them close. Works for me."

There was no hugging before Savannah slipped into her boots and headed for her truck. Just words that echoed in the silence and a slender thread of newfound peace.

Madeline was welcome here. Her family had been part of this valley for generations. Not a big part, not for many years, but no one seemed to be holding any grudges.

This valley wasn't scaring her away at all, with its many feet of snow and the promise of winter blizzards and echoes of loss. More than any other place she'd ever lived in, this place felt like home, and as for the people… she didn't know much about them just yet but one thing she did know.

Flaws and all and she had plenty… they welcomed her with open arms.

MIRACLE OF MIRACLES and with Bette's help, Madeline managed to source triple glazed made-to-measure windows with a guaranteed delivery date the week after Thanksgiving. The look on Seth's face when she'd told him she'd already measured up and put the order in had been priceless, but he hadn't said a word. He'd simply taken her drawings and the order form for the windows and remeasured and recalculated them all over again.

If he found an error, Madeline would be grateful, she

decided as she waited for him to finish. No need to mention that she'd already had it checked by one of Bette's architect consultants and a draftsperson friend besides. If she was the one taking on the fit out of the new windows, she'd be checking every measurement too.

Why he'd ever agreed to doing the work when he so clearly didn't want to and he barely had the time to eat, she didn't know, but he had agreed to it and she was grateful. Even if she was paying through the nose for his trouble.

"What do you want done with the windows we're taking out?"

"No idea. Do you think anyone would want them?"

"I have a buyer."

"Who?"

"Me. I recycle when I can, and I'll give you a fair price for them."

"Done."

"Your calculations are correct."

"What a surprise."

"No one likes a smart-ass, Maddie."

Which as far as she was concerned was his way of saying, *why Madeline, you're doing a great job, I couldn't have done any better myself.* "You do realize that whenever you say that I take it as a win, yes? And pat myself on the back and do all sorts of little internal happy dances?"

"See, that's just plain weird. What do you want done with all those boxes in the hallway?"

"Oh. I—they're just boxes of old clothes that need to go to charity."

"Want me to drop them off for you?"

She nodded, not trusting herself to speak. Darling man.

"What about the hospital bed in the end room? Because I know a family that could use one. They'd pay you for it."

"No! I mean—if someone has a use for it they can have it. I don't want money for it." And really, what other use for that bed could there be other than to make an unwell person a little more comfortable?

"Consider it done."

"Good of you to do them a favor."

"Everyone gets *one*," he muttered, and stalked off to re-measure a floor-to-ceiling drop.

Seriously, what was it with him not wanting to be seen to be doing her any favors? Especially when he was racking them up on a daily basis? "Okay, I'll be in the downstairs bar trying to choose kitchen fittings if you need me."

She hadn't planned on doing anything to the lower level of the house before Christmas. Time was one factor. The fact that it had long ago been established as a gentlemen's retreat and that her father might want it to stay that way was another. Meanwhile, she'd been using it as a design studio, a place to collect all her decorating thoughts in one place.

"You mean the famous Love ranch bar?"

Had she shown him that part of the house yet? She knew his tradespeople had been in there fixing plumbing, but maybe he hadn't. "You want to see it?"

"Don't make me beg."

"I'd definitely like to see you beg."

"Because odes have been written to it, Maddie. Community fundraising committees remain grateful to it. It was the end point of a cross-valley snow ski race some twenty years ago and people still talk about it with love in their hearts. My brother Jett could help set up another cross-country ski race fundraiser with the bar as the finish line if you've a mind to serve the sporting community. He's well connected."

"Your brother Jett… Casey." The name finally clicked. "The Olympic gold medalist."

"That's the one."

Seth sounded proud of his brother's success. How was she supposed to stay unimpressed when he got sweeter *and* sexier every time they met? "How come your family never bought this place all those years ago when it was up for sale? Surely a neighbor would have been a preferred buyer to an out of towner?"

"Couple of reasons. Old Ron Hanks was a widower, no kids, so the place went to nieces and nephews and they weren't from around here. They wanted the place sold to the highest bidder, which brings me to the second reason the hammer landed with your family rather than mine. My family's pockets just weren't deep enough back then."

But his were and he'd worked hard to make them so. They reached the lower level, office, bathroom, and mudrooms to the right, long bar to the left.

"My father brought me here once when I was a kid and it blew me away," he murmured. "You're not going to turn it into an exercise studio or an artist's workroom? I'll weep if you are, but it'll be manly and tough weeping and I'll do it in private."

"I might keep the bar." His eyes lit up, he really was ridiculously attractive when enthusiasm for something held sway. "I might, I don't know, invite all the neighbors around for drinks in between Thanksgiving and Christmas. Ask them to bring copies of any old pictures or newspaper clippings to do with that ski race. Is that the kind of invite people around here would be open to?"

Smiley black eyes could be very compelling, especially when framed with fine laughter lines strong brows and thick black hair. "Very open to."

So now she had a plan to become part of the community here—which might just be a good thing for when her father came to stay. She could be out *doing things*. Festive, social things, wrapped in eggnog and goodwill, and maybe her father and his freshly built family could join in if they wanted to. Rather than her dancing attendance on them, they could choose to be part of her busy, exciting life here.

Visually, the bar was a well-proportioned, solidly designed room with stone features, timber everything else and a bar that ran half the length of one wall. Sky-blue felt on the billiard table—and she wondered how much that little tweak had cost—and the same color picked up again in the light-shades above the table. Antler chandeliers featured heavily in the sitting areas and two huge floor rugs with deep wool pile in all the colors of the ocean graced the floor. There were rustic barstools and deeply comfortable club chairs. She figured there was seating here for fifty, at least, and standing room for another hundred.

Records had shown that the room design had been her grandmother's doing. Part Rockefeller Gilded Age, part mountain lodge, it had weathered very, *very* well.

She didn't want to change anything in here. She liked it exactly as it was.

She slipped behind the bar and studied the shelves laden with hundreds of bottles of spirits and liqueurs. "What can I get for you, sir?" Might as well get into character.

"Ladies' choice." He pulled out a barstool and planted his very fine rear on it. "I'll have what you're having."

She took a bottle from the shelf that she knew would meet his approval, blew some of the dust off and uncapped the lid before lifting it to her nose. Looked like bourbon, smelled like bourbon, did this stuff go off? Wouldn't want to poison anyone. She set the bottle in front of him and went in search of scotch glasses. They were beyond dusty—the cleaning crew hadn't been let loose in here—but there was a sink at the end of the bar and four beer taps up that end too. Several kegs of beer sat in the basement, probably all set to explode. "How long does beer last in a keg?"

"No idea but you could ask at Grey's Saloon or Flint-works in Marietta. They'd know. Fourteen-year-old kegs full of beer sound grim to me. Time to get rid of them." He'd been staring at the shelves full of spirits behind her. "Do you have *any* idea how much some of those bottles behind you are worth?"

"None." She finished washing and rinsing the glasses and shook them as dry as she could before setting them beside the Pappy. "You pour."

"Hell no. Working-class man here, Maddie. Take pity and *you* pour the drinks from the ten-thousand-dollar bottle of booze."

Really? That much? Status symbols were weird. She poured with a heavy hand. "Does it need ice?"

"No!" He winced.

She smiled. Pulling his leg was so much fun.

She sipped and tasted bourbon. He sipped and she waited for him to have an epiphany. "Nice?"

"Yup. Scratch that one off the bucket list."

"You have a bucket list?"

He nodded. "I'm a man of many lists, just ask my office staff. Now where are these kitchen plans? I want to go over them."

She won the fancy kitchen tap war. He won the counter-top debate, mainly because he could source what was needed locally and time was of the essence. She poured more bourbon for them and Seth smiled wide and warm.

"Thanksgiving's coming up soon," she murmured. "Is that a big thing for people around here?" She'd never really observed it. "Is there somewhere a person might go if they didn't want to be alone but didn't want to stand out like a green tree frog in snow?"

"Why don't you join us for Thanksgiving? It'll be a mixture of family and friends, it always is. You should come."

"Oh, no. Thank you." Not quite what she'd had in mind. "I didn't mean to come across as an abandoned waif. I just… I'm missing seeing lots of people around. Not necessarily people I know. Just people in general. I'm aiming to get into Marietta more now that I'm settled in out here. That'll fix it."

"Will it?" he asked sceptically.

"Trust me, I have always been a loner. That's nothing new. Except that this time round I thought I'd try for a little bit… more."

He was looking at her strangely again. "There's a difference between being a loner and being lonely," he offered finally. "My big brother's a loner. That's not you."

"Lonely, then," she acknowledged crossly. "How come I let you call me out on all my crap but you disappear every time I start to say thanks for helping?"

He smirked and tapped his almost empty glass. "You know the rules, Maddie."

Any deep and meaningful conversation between them required fair warning and apparently three measures of very old, very fancy bourbon. "If I pour you another drink will you tell me why you have a hang-up about being seen to do me any favors?"

"You're probably going to hear about it anyway if you ever meet the rest of the family. Which you probably will."

She shrugged and poured. "Spill."

"I met a woman when I was twenty-three. She was older, divorced, and had the helpless act down to a fine art. I fell in love with her, spent all my spare time fixing up the big old house she'd bought with her divorce settlement. I finished the house, got it looking like a million bucks. I'd even started looking for a ring to put on her finger." He picked up his glass and took a hefty swig. "Forgive me, Pappy, but baring my soul ain't easy," he murmured.

But he was doing it. That was the part she found astonishing. He was telling her about his failures and secrets because she'd asked.

"And I came in one day—I was practically living with her by then—and she said thank you, Seth, for all your fine work and all the favors you've done for me this past year while I found my feet, but I sold the house today for three times what I bought it for and I'm out of here. It's been nice knowing ya."

"That *bitch*." Could be the liquor talking. "How dare she!"

"Exactly." But he was smiling, just a little bit. "She preyed on my—"

"Soft and tender heart and really hot body?"

"I was going to say *affections*." He moved the bottle away from her as if she was going to start swilling from it. "I was gutted but I learned a good lesson. No more endless favors. One's my limit."

"And are you still in love with her?" It seemed important that she know.

"No. I got over her a long time ago."

"Do I remind you of her?" That seemed important to know too.

"No. But you are a little…" He stopped abruptly.

She waited ever so patiently.

"Aren't you going to interrupt?" he asked finally.

"No." It was an excellent no. It had heft. "I am a little *what?*"

"Out of your depth here. And I like being needed, so that's why you only get one favor. So you don't start relying on me to save you, and we don't go starting anything stupid."

"Stupid…" she echoed. Made perfect sense. He was, in every sense of the word, quite stupid, and she definitely didn't need to go starting anything with a stupid man. "You're so right."

He nodded sagely. "I usually am."

"But even if I am out of my depth here, I'm resilient. I've worked hard to become so. Whatever life throws at me, I roll with the punches. It's a signature move of mine."

He snorted and she splashed some more poppy, pappy,

whatever, into his glass and added a little more to her glass too. "And I'm not little," she said indignantly. "Look at me. I'm meaty."

"Slender as a reed," he muttered.

"Sturdy. Robust."

"Tall is all. But I'm taller." He was also smug. "Tell you what I'm going to do. I'm going to take you to Grey's Saloon for a meal this Friday night and introduce you round so you get to know everyone and then someone will say what are you doing for Thanksgiving, Madd-ee, and you'll say nothing and then ten people will invite you over to watch the game, which means I won't be sitting around wondering if you're all lonely up here all by yourself."

"So... by inviting me out to dinner you'll be doing *yourself* a favor."

"Exactly."

"Not me a favor."

"Nope."

Made sense.

"What the hell alcohol percentage is this bourbon anyway?" He picked up the bottle and squinted at the label.

"Can you see it?" she asked, although definitely not in a needy way. More of a curious, robustly resilient kind of way. "Because this stuff's probably not supposed to send you blind."

"Up to fifty... three... percent. Might explain it."

"Explain what?"

He leaned forward across the scarred and time-bitten bar. "This burning need I have to…"

She leaned forward too, no point keeping her distance given his burning need to confess—

His lips met hers, warm and mobile, gently coaxing, utterly perfect. *He* was perfect and she was inexplicably, delightfully lost.

She had been kissed before, a bit. Half-heartedly, apparently, although she hadn't realized it at the time.

Because she'd never been kissed like *this*.

There was yearning in this kiss, a searching quest for pleasure and connection, all of it wrapped in the sweetness of smoky bourbon. He was all-in, putting himself out there for the tasting, and she'd never been anyone's *all-in* before and it was intoxicating.

"You're out of your depth," he whispered against her lips, and maybe she was.

But the way she saw it… She paused to collect another magic kiss or two before replying. "Seth…"

So many feelings wrapped up in one word, and maybe this was her carving out a place for him in her heart alongside the ghosts of the past and the uncertainties her father presented. Not a life raft in a sea of uncertainty but an opportunity, brightly beckoning.

"You're right. I am totally out of my depth here with you," she confessed, because truth telling demanded honesty in return. "But I'm willing to learn."

Chapter Eight

S ETH CASEY WASN'T a man to make false promises. He'd told Maddie he'd take her out for dinner and take her out he would. Didn't mean he couldn't call for reinforcements. Didn't mean he wouldn't call in favors in the interests of not making a complete fool of himself.

So what if he spent more time out at her place than was strictly necessary? So what if he pulled his best tradesmen off other jobs to see to Madeline's needs? It was worth it to see the old ranch house gleaming again, even if the place didn't belong to him, he told himself magnanimously. He was being well paid for his trouble so there was no parallel at all with what had happened all those years ago when he was young and stupid.

Madeline wasn't using him. She liked him, that was it.

And he liked her.

There was a simplicity to that notion. No need to overthink it.

So here he was, trying to figure out how to ask two of his favorite people to drop by Grey's Saloon tonight while he and Maddie were there so they could meet her, get to know her, because somehow that had become important to him if he wanted to take things any further.

And he really, really wanted to proceed.

He came back to the kitchen conversation with a jolt when Jett snorted into his coffee and then choked on it. Classy. But Mardie was smirking at *him* not Jett, and his niece was eyeing him with the wounded disappointment only a preschooler could conjure. "What've I done?"

"You mean apart from talk about a woman's way with up-lighting for twenty minutes solid?" said his brother. "Not that I know what that means. Also, you're ignoring your niece's purple-haired pony."

He looked down at the purple plastic pony currently grazing his kneecaps. Uncle duties sadly neglected. "That is one fine horse." He watched in bemusement as his niece neighed and then she and the purple-haired pony galloped away. Greener pastures elsewhere and all that, he figured. He really should get her a plastic handyman kit. Or a little front-end loader she could sit in, with push pedals or an electric engine. Best uncle ever.

"When do we get to meet her?"

Now would be the perfect time to cajole them into dropping by the saloon later this evening for introductions. Although look at that sky… If he mentioned it, they'd feel obliged to make the effort and anyone with eyes could see the weather was closing in.

"He's gone again," said Jett.

"What?" He was right here. "Tonight. I said I'd take her to Grey's for a meal and introduce her around to people tonight. You could join us for a meal or drop by for a drink if you want to meet her. I like her," he said. "And it's not about the house." And surely that was *enough*. "She's an interior designer and I *still* like her." Very telling, that.

Mardie had started smirking again. "Since when has he been on board with interior designers of any kind?" she asked Jett. "Remember the floating couch argument?"

"How could anyone forget?"

"I stand by my opinion that sticking a couch in the middle of a room means people are going to fall over it. Besides, it was dark." Seth might not have been wholly awake at the time. "I needed stitches!"

"Speaking of," said Jett. "Mason and Cal almost ripped each other a new one last night, and they did it at the Bearback Bar in Bozeman."

Seth could feel his shoulders curl in as he contemplated the seething mass of resentments and attitude his two older brothers had taken to airing in public. "Someone's gonna have to sort that out soon." But he couldn't see a solution. The ranch only needed one manager. A manager and a couple of ranch hands, and when their father had been alive that was how it had worked. His father at the top and Cal and Mason doing the grunt work.

"Cara's back in Marietta and looking for a property investments manager," said Mardie.

Seth laughed, he couldn't help it. "Mason's too stubborn and proud to go after Cara again. Not when she's flashing all the cash. As for him being employed by her, forget it. Never going to happen."

Widowed Cara Sefton-Blair, the kid whose parents had barely been able to clothe her, was now wealthy beyond measure courtesy of her late transport-logistics husband. She'd been Mason's high school sweetheart but had lit out for Texas without so much as a goodbye the day after she'd finished school. She'd returned recently, but gossip could be cruel, and she hadn't fared well. "Isn't she going back to Texas at some point?"

"Nope," said Mardie, popping the *P* in nope. "She's living at the Graff, taking beauty treatments every other day and looking for investment opportunities. Last week, she bought her parents a summer house down Yellowstone way. The week before that she bought a ski lodge in Kalispell and a cherry farm on Flathead Lake. She's looking to buy a ranch in Paradise Valley."

Smart real estate, all of it.

"She and Madeline hit it off when Maddie was staying at the Graff," pressed Mardie. "Maybe, given that Madeline's looking to get to know people, we could all end up at dinner tonight, Cara included. And if Madeline in all her innocence gets Cara to open up about why she left Marietta and why she's back, wouldn't that be worth knowing?"

"I don't like it." Seth knew that much. "We start hanging out with Cara for whatever reason and Mason's going to see it as a betrayal." He turned to his brother. "You *know* this."

Jett scratched his head, a sure sign of unease.

"If Mason wants Cara back, I'll welcome her with open arms but not before." Seth didn't know how to explain his position to his sister-in-law. "And that's not to say you can't be friends with Cara all you want or that your instincts aren't good when it comes to what social situations might get us more information, but I won't be party to putting Mason in a situation he's not ready for. I can call him an idiot all I like—and do—but I won't go behind his back."

"I hear you," said Mardie. "I get it. He's your brother."

NERVOUSNESS TOOK HOLD of Madeline as she approached Grey's Saloon in Marietta. Seth was in there somewhere and this wasn't a date, never mind the memory of sweet bourbon kisses. He'd called her a couple of times so far this week but only to discuss house renovations and materials he wanted to order. He'd been friendly, professional, neighborly, and perfectly willing to carry on as if he hadn't kissed her at all and that was awkward as all hell given she'd gladly accept more.

More kissing. Actual dating instead of some sort of introductions-all-round evening, which was nice of him, of course it was, and she should be thankful, and she *was*.

Smile, Madeline. Check your appearance in the reflective glass of a nearby shop window and get ready to be judged. Heels together, knees together, make sure you look all put together, even if you're only wearing jeans and a sweater and a magenta fine wool coat. Tuck your hair back behind one ear, the better to see your mother's art deco earrings that will definitely bring good luck, and go and be present in the moment and place in time. Maybe you'll find a friend, a whole roomful of friends. Maybe you won't.

"You'll never know unless you turn up," she murmured. She'd driven all this way on dark icy roads just to be here and that had been an adventure in itself. "So turn up."

"Madeline?" Footsteps came to a stop behind her and she turned to see the woman she'd met in the bar at the Graff when she'd first arrived in Marietta. "I thought it was you. It's Cara. We met at—"

"The hotel bar," Madeline finished for her.

"You okay?" Cara asked. "You look a little lost."

"No, I'm heading for that place right there so that a new friend can introduce me to more potential new friends and I'm not great at making a good first impression, or second impression, let's be honest, so I stopped for a little pep talk."

"Well, you look gorgeous."

"Thank you. So do you." Cara's severe black high-waist trousers, crop top and snow-white coat fairly screamed couture. "Vera Wang?"

Cara nodded and spread her arms wide. "You like?"

"Love it." Maybe she'd misjudged her own clothing choices—maybe Grey's Saloon was a high-fashion paradise—but it was too late to do anything about that now.

"How do you like living out at your ranch?" A friendly question, polite. Good memory for the only other conversation they'd ever had.

"It's a lot different to Manhattan."

Cara laughed. "That it is. C'mon. Let's get you inside so you can meet all these friends of friends and wow them with your good self."

They entered the bar together, a waft of warm air, food smells, and loud conversation washing over her. "Wow. Is it always this busy in here?"

"Friday night," said Cara.

"Table for two?" asked a waitress just as Madeline spotted Seth, and Mardie his sister-in-law and another dark-haired man who, given his resemblance to Seth, was probably his married-to-Mardie brother.

"No, I'm meeting friends. I can see them already at that table over there."

The young waitress followed her gaze. "Table for Casey, head on over. And you, ma'am?"

Cara smiled as she shrugged out of her coat, her inky-black hair spilling every which way, a perfect foil against her white coat and porcelain skin. "I'm just here to have a drink and make a point of being seen."

The server didn't bat an eye. "Seat for one at the bar?"

"Perfect."

It didn't sound perfect to Madeline. "Um, would you like to join us? In the interest of meeting people and making friends?"

Cara looked toward Seth's table and a flat smile stole all the animation from her face. "We've history, me and the Caseys, and joining you tonight is not a good idea. But if you ever do want to catch up, give me a call at the Graff. We'll do lunch or a trip to the hot springs or you can invite me out to your beautiful home and show me around."

"I'd like that." Making friends was easy here. "I will call."

"Aw, sweet pea." Madeline found herself enveloped in a warm hug and a waft of magnolia perfume. "I won't hold you to that. Now go be you."

Seth had his head in his hands by the time she reached the table and Maddie sought Mardie's input for reassurance, silently flicking her gaze to him and back with a question in her eyes that she hoped didn't need any accompanying words.

"Don't mind him," said Mardie cheerfully. "He was just witnessing the oracle that is me. He'll come good eventually. Meanwhile, this is my husband, Jett. The handsome one I was telling you about. I never lie."

"I see that."

"Pleased to meet you, Madeline." Jett offered up a charming smile and a relaxed confidence she immediately warmed to. "Seth tells me you're an interior design whiz."

"He does?" At least the man in question had lowered his hands from his face.

"Hey, Maddie. Come and meet my brother. And you somehow know Mardie."

"I do."

Seth smiled as Madeline slid into the booth beside him. There was plenty of room—the booth could have happily seated six. And it seemed only sensible to put her handbag and coat between them on the bench seat, but she didn't want to. Better all round to tuck her coat and bag under her legs and hope the floor hadn't had a recent encounter with spilled food and ketchup. She smiled and slid in a little further along the bench—in a move she could only hope they didn't interpret as forward. "You look very handsome."

His shirt was plain black, but the buttons were fancy and the collar was a classic one, no casual button-down for him, even if the couple of buttons left open at the neck gave him an air of informality. He'd swapped his father's battered old work watch for an elegant silver dress watch on a black leather band. Or, given the name on the dial, it could have been platinum.

"Mardie," she murmured. "I'm lodging a protest. I think this one here's in the running for handsomest Casey brother." Her words were firmly tongue in cheek given they were both so easy on the eye and shared a certain similarity of build and bone structure.

"Eye of the beholder," said Mardie airily, with a wave of her hand. "Wait until you see all five of them together. It's Marlboro Man central."

That was the start of an evening filled with salty fries and onion rings, thick steaks and new names and faces as Seth made good on his promise and introduced her to so many people she eventually lost count.

She wasn't the life of the party by any means. Some of the people were more interested in who her father was than who she was, but she was an old hand at that dynamic by now and navigated her way through those conversations deftly enough.

It wasn't until she went to the restroom and shut herself in a spacious toilet cubicle that she got a taste of the gossip that had likely been circulating all night. It came in the form of two women talking about Seth—and her—as they assessed his looks, his bank balance, and his clearly well-known desire to buy her ranch.

"What's his deal with her?" one of the women said. "Did you see the look he sent Boyd? Even though he was the one who introduced them to begin with. He's been introducing her around all night as if he's inviting people to step in and take her off his hands. Is he into her or not?"

"Maybe he's hedging his bets. Waiting to see if she'll sell him that ranch, no strings attached. If that happens, he doesn't have to pretend to be into her at all."

"And if she doesn't sell?"

"Guess he'll have to marry her for it."

Both women laughed and left the bathroom shortly thereafter, leaving Madeline sick to her stomach at their words. Only once she thought the bathroom was completely empty did she emerge to wash her hands. There was one other person still in a cubicle and she hurried so she wouldn't have to face them, but she wasn't that lucky. The door opened and the woman's eyes met hers.

Cara.

Cara took a basin two over from the one Madeline was using. "You know, when I was a dirt-poor little girl, I thought money could solve any problem," Cara said. "I wanted to be rich so bad I didn't care who I hurt along the way. It's only after you have more money than you can ever spend that you realize that money brings a whole new set of problems, especially for women who have it and men who don't." She grabbed a paper towel from a dispenser on the wall and wiped her hands and turned back to the mirror to refresh her lipstick. "For what it's worth I don't think Seth's the type to pretend an interest in you that isn't there. He's not going to marry you for your ranch."

"But he does want it," Madeline felt compelled to point out.

"So? I saw a Rembrandt I wanted the other day, but I didn't buy it. I can buy other paintings in this world that I don't have to sell my soul for."

"Maybe you're more enlightened than other people."

Madeline watched as the other woman expertly reapplied her lipstick and touched up her mascara.

Maybe Cara had already sold her soul.

"Seth's into you. Just you. He's bringing you into his world to see what you make of it. To help you decide whether or not you want *him*. And you can choose to believe me, or you can choose to believe those gossips but I'm the one who's right."

Confidence, thy name was Cara.

"You can't know what's in a man's heart just by looking at him," Madeline countered.

"True, but I've known Seth since he was a kid. I used to hang out with his big brother Mason, and that's a whole 'nother story I figure you'll hear if you decide to stick around." Cara headed for the door. "Seth's no gold digger. Do yourself a favor and believe it."

MADELINE RETURNED TO the table now full of yet more people to get to know—Seth was absolutely living up to his promise to introduce her around—and she called on her schooling and made small talk and lasted another hour or more, but the luster had gone out of the evening. Eventually, she turned to Seth and Mardie and Jett and told them she was calling it a night. Snow had started falling outside, fat flakes drifting gently to the ground and there was more on the way—she'd checked the weather report before she'd left the ranch.

"I can follow you home if you like," offered Seth. "Or drop you home and have one of my guys drive your car out in the morning."

But she shook her head and smiled and chose to believe he had no ulterior motive for being nice to her. "No need. I decided on the way in that I'd be staying at the Graff tonight so I can shop in the morning. My car's already parked there. But you can walk me there if you like? I wouldn't say no to that."

She knew the way. She'd already walked it once, but it wouldn't hurt to have company.

This is me, choosing to believe that you like spending time with me. Thank you, Cara. Thank you, psychologists one, two, and three.

The walk back to the hotel was largely a silent one. Madeline was all talked out and Seth made no move to cut the companionable silence. When she skidded on an icy patch, he said nothing, merely took her hand and tucked it into the crook of his arm and kept right on walking. Only when they came to a halt beneath the hotel portico did he speak.

"I know it can be a lot, coming out on the town with me. I have a big family and you haven't met the half of them. I know a lot of people through my work. Come summer, I can have six or seven crews running and I try to keep in touch. I hope tonight wasn't too much for you. I was kinda hoping to break you in gently."

"I'm not really very outgoing." No surprises there. "I'm better with small groups than large, or one-on-one, you might have noticed. But I did enjoy myself this evening and I do want to thank you for the invite."

"So polite," he said with a crooked smile. "Do you mean it? 'Cause you looked a little wobbly there a couple of times."

"Wobbles are expected when you're me. They're character building."

"I like your character," he said gruffly.

And she liked his. On impulse, she leaned in and pressed a gentle kiss to his cheek surprising a smile out of him and a discreet cough from the nearby doorman. "Good night, Seth."

"Yeah," he said and stood his ground as she pulled away because she could hardly stand around staring into his eyes all night and she wasn't yet ready to invite him in. "It is."

Chapter Nine

THANKSGIVING WASN'T QUITE as challenging a day as Christmas, to Madeline's way of thinking but it was challenging enough. She'd grown used to spending it alone, never mind her repeated attempts to connect with her father at some point during the day. She'd grown used to *thinking* her thanks rather than saying it out loud.

Thank you for this beautiful house and all the treasured memories that live within it. Thank you for my health, my life, and so many daily blessings.

She'd made plans, this Thanksgiving, and they were solo plans, but she was aiming for a fun and fruitful day of learning. Right after she made her traditional contact with her father.

She'd started off with phone calls, but he'd rarely picked up.

As a teenager she'd written him letters, but he'd never written back.

For a couple of years there she'd moved onto emails but they'd probably gone to spam.

These days she got all dressed up, full makeup and hair,

and used her phone and halo lighting to make a video message that went straight to his phone. Last year he'd even written HAPPY THANKSGIVING back.

Never let it be said that give or take a thousand years or so, water couldn't carve rock.

She dressed carefully, no digging into the family jewels today, opting instead for the diamond tennis bracelet her father had given her for her sixteenth birthday and the big pink teardrop pearl earrings she'd bought for herself on her twenty-first. She got a little daring with a pale pink velvet dress with wide shoulder straps and a shimmery pewter-colored, long-sleeved tee underneath and figured she could blame it on solitary-mountain living if need be.

She'd grown used to the idea that her father never pressed play on her messages anyway.

It was kinda liberating.

"Hey, Dad, happy Thanksgiving. I just wanted to call to say thank you so much for holding onto this place while I grew up and for giving me the opportunity to reconnect with it as an adult. These mountains are crazy beautiful and so is this home. I hope you like what I've done with it."

She stood behind a chair in her mother's sunroom, and instead of a hospital bed she'd added outrageous textured wallpaper etched with swirling florals and velvet club chairs in deepest bronze and stacks of books and a bigger table for jigsaw puzzles and a sideboard displaying a porcelain tea set in butter-yellow stripes. It was her English high tea room in the middle of Montana. Fresh, feminine, and over-the-top ridiculous. All it lacked was a vase full of blowsy roses and she'd already put in a standing weekly order for some with the florist, beginning next week. She smiled for the video, spontaneous and unscripted.

"I've been going through Mom's stuff and Grandma Peggy's things too and it's been so cathartic. Did you know they collected artwork? Well, I'm sure you did but I never knew. Some of it is so beautiful and expensive too because I have all the notes of sale. So if there are any pieces here that you want, that you remember, just let me know. Or you can take a look when you come for Christmas. I'm so looking forward to that, and to meeting the people you hold dear."

She wanted to be kind to them and to him. "I'm growing wise here in this valley. Montana does that to you, I think. I'm beginning to figure out what I want and how to love. How to move on. So thank you for keeping this place safe for me. And for giving me so much. I love you, Dad. Happy Thanksgiving. I hope wherever you are that it's a good one."

Don't overthink it, don't replay or edit, just send.

And... done.

She knew better than to think she'd hear back from him, but she had a busy day ahead and headed first for the bedroom to change into more practical clothes and then to the kitchen, which hadn't yet been renovated but she was getting used to working with what was there and the knowledge that her mother and grandmother had cooked in this kitchen didn't hurt either.

Today was about conquering the big wood fuel stove and trialing new recipes. She was cooking up a feast, one she hoped to replicate on Christmas Day. Big turkey full of stuffing, lots of clever sides, and pecan pie to finish. She'd even made a flowchart telling her what to prepare and when. Give or take five hours then she'd have enough cooked deliciousness to last for a week. She'd taken cooking lessons in Switzerland at finishing school but there was no denying that many of those lessons had been about crafting a dinner menu that someone else would cook. She had been taught how to make the very good eggs Benedict though. Probably so that if her bedroom skills were mediocre she could still whip up a little something special at breakfast the next morning. Apparently, this worked to secure husbands for upper-class women the world over.

Apparently, isolated Montana valley living was making her cynical as well as grateful. Not too cynical, she hoped, as she stuffed slender pieces of dry wood in the stove's firebox along with paper and kindling, made sure all the flue parts were wide open, and lit a match.

No instant heat for this old girl. She'd gone online and read all the directions. Getting a wood stove up and running required patience.

There was one other phone call she wanted to make, and it didn't have to *mean* anything unless Seth wanted it to mean something. He could read it as a client simply being polite if he wanted to. She didn't mean to push for a relationship.

She didn't know *how* to push for a relationship, although maybe it was something she could learn. A bit like Christmas cooking.

"Hey, Seth." It was her day for reaching out and getting answering machines in return. "It's Madeline. Madeline Love." As if in the space of a day he'd completely forgotten who she was. She screwed up her face and soldiered on in the face of her stupidity. "I'm just calling to say how grateful I am for all your goodwill and all the extra work you're putting in on my account. Helping me hang all the artwork definitely went above and beyond." Her chance of ever getting him to do that particular job ever again was zero. "So, thank you again. You're an awesome, handsome, very useful individual. And, er... kissing." *What was she saying?* "Grateful for the kissing, too."

She ended the call and fumbled the phone in horror before letting it clatter to the counter and pushing it as far away from her as possible.

You did not just do that.

But she had.

Wood. Surely the fire in the stove needed more wood. Best get on that.

Anything to distract her from what she'd just done.

Chapter Ten

S ETH DIDN'T UNDERSTAND why instead of turning off at the entrance to the family ranch he kept right on driving, all the way up to Madeline's place. He called it that now. Maddie's place, to remind himself that someone had finally taken ownership of the Love ranch, and it wasn't him.

She was doing the homestead proud, and it pleased him. She was the best interior designer he'd ever seen. And it wasn't just because the house had great bones or because she seemed to have an endless supply of high-end furniture and paintings. It was because she knew exactly where to put everything so that a space became warm and inviting. Interesting. Whenever he turned up to work on the home, he enjoyed every moment and had a hard time leaving.

He should have been watching the game with his brothers. Football was serious business around here and he could have been cussing and bonding and putting a beer to his lips.

But here he stood, knocking on Madeline's door without any invitation in place, not sure of his welcome but unable to forget a kiss he should never have stolen in the first place. Or the next kiss on his cheek after a night out with his friends and family. A night where even he hadn't been able to dodge the rumors that he was only interested in her assets. More specifically, that he wanted her ranch and was not above marrying her to get it.

He hated that some people thought that way about him. That on the building site some of his guys had taken to teasing him about it. How did a boss speak to that notion without completely losing his shit and roaring, *Nonono, I fucking like her, you pissants, and the next person who calls me a gold digger is fired?*

Although... that might just work.

He was still contemplating the merits and possible fallout from so loudly declaring his feelings when Madeline's door jerked abruptly open to reveal her.

Which was odd, because as far as he was concerned, he hadn't even rung the door buzzer yet.

"Hey," he said. Brilliant conversationalist that he was.

"Seth!" Was that relief in her voice? And why? "You are such a godsend! I need your help."

And then she was reaching out to grab him by the arm, dragging him inside and letting him go way too soon in favor of leading the way through the foyer and atrium living area at a fast enough clip to make him frown.

To call her kitchen a mess was an understatement. Pots and pans, bowls and utensils littered every countertop but the main problem, the way he saw it, was the happily smoking woodstove and inescapable smell of burning food.

"I did everything the recipe said but the turkey cooked so fast and now it's too hot to handle and too big to lift out of the oven without getting burned and I think something is on fire in there anyway and not just the wood."

As far as summaries went, it was a good one. "Got it." He looked around for the poker or a little shovel that might help him reposition firewood but there was nothing in sight. Her kitchen tongs were tiny. If she had a kitchen fire extinguisher, he couldn't see it. "Got any kitchen gloves?"

She pointed to a smouldering mess in the ashes of the unlit open fireplace.

"How about towels?" he asked.

In the end they used a bunch of folded dishcloths and between them they got the bird out of the oven and onto a metal grate he'd set up in the fireplace in the hope the fumes would head up the chimney and out of the house. He relieved the stove of a few too many cords of wood and deftly covered them in the ashy remains of an earlier fire.

Together they stared at the blackened smoking remains of the world's largest turkey.

"Well done," he said.

"Sure is." She sighed heavily. "It's possible I put too much wood in the stove."

"Looks like." He couldn't stop his smile so he tried to hide it by rubbing his hand across his jaw. "Could be." Not entirely her fault. "Temperamental bastards, wood stoves. Takes a while to get the hang of them." He looked at the remaining chaos. "Who are you expecting over?"

"Huh?" She looked momentarily confused and so pretty, standing there all flushed and messy, with her hair pulled back in a haphazard ponytail and pretty pink pearl bobbles dangling from her ears. "Oh. No one. I'm having a Christmas food practice run so that nothing goes wrong on the day."

"Smart." He nodded. Tried not to glance at the chaos.

"I'll try again next week."

She had more try in her than anyone he knew. Maybe that was what made her so irresistible. "Who is coming here for Christmas again?"

"My father, his new fiancée, who I've never met, and my seven-year-old half-brother who I've also never met. And hopefully my old boss Bette if I can promise to find her a cowboy to dance with afterward." She turned away, hiding her face from him. "I want to make a good impression."

That was quite some list of people she'd never met. Why did he always want to know more about her than she revealed? Why did he always want to make her smile? And wipe the floor with anyone who didn't make her smile?

"Anyway..." She struggled to fill space his silence had left. "What can I do for you?"

"Do you want to have Thanksgiving with us? And by us, I mean me and my family."

"You've asked me this before."

He couldn't deny it. He also knew her a little better this

time round. "Try, try again," he explained. "I'm a believer." He could sense the refusal on her lips. "Besides, my mother sent me up here to say that if you didn't want to stay for the meal you could still drop in anytime on your way to or from somewhere else." His mother had done no such thing, but she wasn't the kind to fuss when it came to having another mouth to feed, especially at Thanksgiving. "Very neighborly." That much was true.

"I can't turn up empty-handed," she said next, and maybe she had a point there. She could have turned up empty-handed where his mother's Thanksgiving table was concerned but people usually didn't. They turned up with sides, sweets, snacks, drinks—all of those were fair game. And sure, Madeline had a cellar full of rare wines and a bar groaning with expensive liquor but she also had a mountain of fresh food sitting on the counter that needn't go to waste.

He picked up a bunch of asparagus out of the six or so bunches sitting in a box. He wasn't a terrible cook and as luck would have it, he knew what to do with these. "Do you trust me?"

"With my asparagus?"

"Yes, with your asparagus." He could start there and work his way up to gaining her trust full stop. "Do you have plans for them?"

"I'm supposed to blanch them in boiling water for a minute and then toss them in a mustard and citrus reduction. Then I add mushrooms and serve them at room temperature."

They didn't have all day. "Get some water boiling, I'll do my frypan special to go with it."

Butter, garlic paste, lemon juice, salt and pepper, and a squeeze of honey, with Madeline hovering at his shoulder and watching his every move. "Did you make that cranberry sauce?" he asked, looking at a sticky, burnt mess in a saucepan on the counter. "Is it edible?"

"Who would know?" But she fished a teaspoon from a drawer and dipped it in the middle of the pot where the colors still glowed red rather than black and handed him the spoon which he promptly stuck in his mouth.

Not bad, not bad at all, so some of that went in the pan too and by the time he was tipping the third batch of asparagus spears into the fancy red serving dish, he had the mix down to a fine art.

"I have slivered roasted almonds," she said, pointing to another bowl on the counter. "I did those before the oven turned into the gateway to hell."

So they added some of those and a few cranberries just to pretty it all up, and she was looking at him as if he'd just scored the winning touchdown. "I get that look a lot," he murmured.

"I bet you do."

"It usually doesn't last," he warned, and her lilting laughter made him smile that little bit wider in reply. "*Now* will you join us for Thanksgiving?"

"Wearing what I have on? I don't think so."

He made a show of glancing at his watch. He wasn't that late. Yet. But he would be soon if they didn't get a move on. "You've got five minutes."

She stared around her wreck of a kitchen. "Leave it," he warned. "It's not going anywhere. And that turkey's coming with me. You're going to have to get rid of it and it can't go outside."

"It can't?"

"Unless you want to attract wildlife scavengers to the area—which you don't. Go change clothes if you must. I'll take care of the bird."

By the time she returned, he had the trash sorted and the side dish covered with foil and sitting in the back seat of his truck. He didn't head back inside, just stood by his truck, hands in his coat pockets, and waited, trying not to wallow in the deep sense of satisfaction that had come over him.

When Madeline appeared with a wooden crate that she had to set down before closing her big double front doors, he moved to collect it before she had to pick it up again. Wine bottles, they looked like. Half a dozen fusty, dusty bottles of, okay, maybe not wine but definitely liquor, and by the time they pulled up alongside all the other vehicles in front of his family ranch house and she went to collect everything, he couldn't help but speak up.

"You don't need that much," he advised quietly. "It's not about the money or the things you can provide. It's about you putting yourself out there and letting us get to know you. Just being here is enough."

Why that made her tear up was anyone's guess and he leaned in and grabbed the food on the off chance she might pull herself together before his boisterous family got hold of her. He walked toward the door, hoping she'd follow, and heard the door of his truck close and footsteps hurrying to catch up to him.

She had a bottle of wine in each hand when he opened the front door and stood aside to let her in, and her shiny eyes were gone, thank the Lord.

"I can't be empty-handed," she offered, and then they were in his mother's kitchen and Mardie spotted him and moments later so did her daughter. Claire came running toward him full tilt, and he knew how this usually went, and it involved tossing her high in the air as her purple pony toy tried to plant kisses on him.

"Whoa, Claire. Food. Food in hand."

Until Mardie swooped in and took the dish and then it was Claire in the air time as the little girl giggled and pressed a plastic purple pony to his face while yelling, *thank you, thank youuuu*, at the top of her lungs.

"Help," he muttered. "Monster on the loose. Help!" And to his mother, "Maddie made the asparagus."

"Thank you for inviting me to join you, Mrs. Casey." Madeline put the wine on the counter and smiled awkwardly. "It's very kind of you."

Seth didn't miss the very level glance his mother directed his way, or Mardie's undignified snort, but his mother rallied, as he'd known she would.

"It's Savannah, remember? And this is my daughter-in-law Mardie and granddaughter Claire."

"And Wobbles!" Claire twisted so far out of his grasp in order to get to Madeline that Seth almost dropped her.

"You break her, you fix her," said Jett as he too entered the room, but Maddie had already moved in and somehow ended up with an armful of little girl, even if her quiet *oof* conveyed that Claire's landing had probably included a knee to the solar plexus. "Hey, Maddie," said his ever-so-casual brother. "Good to see you again."

Maddie nodded her reply but couldn't quite see past the purple pony in her face. "Hello, Wobbles." Maddie eyeballed Claire next. "Are you a monkey?"

"I'm a horse," the little girl proudly declared.

"My mistake." Madeline repositioned the girl, the better not to drop her. "What's your name?"

"Ploddy."

"I should have guessed. Ploddy and Wobbles, yes."

"Here, let me take your coat." Seth moved in behind Madeline as she awkwardly shrugged out of it, getting a glimpse of a pink velvet tunic that clung to her slender behind. She wore fitted black trousers and knee-high tan boots with a chunky heel and she'd redone her ponytail to look effortlessly elegant. "Mom, can I put some rubbish in the cold room until I leave?"

His mother nodded and turned her attention to his brother. "Jett, honey, can you finish setting the table for me? We're almost ready to eat." By that, Seth figured she meant, *Jett, could you set another place at the table for our unexpected guest, and find an extra chair from somewhere and all the rest.*

"I'll help!" Mardie jumped up.

"Everything you need is in the dresser," his mother called after her.

By the time he got back, Madeline had a drink in her hand, Jett and Claire had disappeared, and Tomas's wife Rowan had joined them in the kitchen.

"Shoo," his mother told him. "We're talking Christmas trees in New York City. You can introduce Madeline to your brothers once they're not glued to the TV screen."

"Who's ahead in the game?"

"Cowboys," said Rowan, and that was just plain disappointing.

"Or I could stay here and get the lowdown on New York City Christmas trees." Because that might be important someday.

"Make yourself useful, then, and come and stir the gravy."

"Yes, ma'am," he told his mother. With Maddie within easy view, he was exactly where he wanted to be.

MADELINE DIDN'T KNOW if it was loneliness, the general theme of gratitude, or the free-flowing wine and abundance of food that made her sink into the evening with childlike abandon but sink she did.

This was a thousand times better than spending the day alone.

Watching Seth at ease in his natural habitat. The way he indulged Claire and willingly took his turn soothing Rowan and Tomas's little cowbaby.

He was closest to his younger brothers, or so it seemed, and he absolutely worshipped his mother—they all did—and that, more than anything, won Madeline over to thinking the best of all of them.

Mothers should be treasured.

And absent fathers remembered in prayer before the meal.

Savannah spoke quietly, thanking her husband for the gift of the growing family they'd created. Savannah thanked every single one of the people around the table for being there, for making her world a better place.

She thanked Madeline for being such a good neighbor—which, hardly—and for taking a chance on getting to know Seth and his band of brothers. She said she hoped her rowdy family didn't scare Madeline away.

Madeline met Seth's bright, inquiring gaze with dimples and a smile she couldn't hide, because his mother's words sounded like a blessing upon her and a warning for Seth and his brothers.

Approval, and she basked in it.

Maybe she had a praise kink.

The conversation turned to Christmas gifts and a mention of Jett buying Claire a set of miniature skis—for which he received teasing from, oh, everyone except her.

"I remember having a toboggan when I was a kid but not skis. What's the age when kids make that transition? I need to know." She had a seven-year-old half-brother to buy for. All suggestions welcome.

"Well, if you're Jett, there isn't one," said Mardie. "His aim is to give Claire all things snow as soon as possible."

"So, if a boy is seven or eight and from the city, where do I start when it comes to all things snow?"

"Snowboard," said Jett.

"Toboggan," said his mother firmly. "Some kids are more timid than others. Just because none of you lot were careful as kids, doesn't mean careful kids don't exist."

Sharing was caring, right? And this family had been sharing themselves with her all night. "My brother—half-brother—is coming for Christmas and I have to get him a gift but not just any gift. It has to be a gift he'll love, a gift to make memories with. I'm open to suggestions."

"I have an idea," said Rowan, who'd parked her shyness somewhere as the evening progressed. "They have these little Polaroid printers that you connect to your phone. If he has a phone, and I'm guessing he will, he can take pictures during the day and print them out later. They're really fun."

"Says the photographer," said her husband affectionately.

"I love that idea." Madeline was all-in. "Toboggan, possibly skis. Polaroid printer. What else?"

"What does he like to do?" asked Savannah, and Madeline's bravado faltered because she didn't know, she'd never met the boy or his mother.

"I'm… not sure. I have this ridiculous inclination to throw everything I can at him and let him choose."

"Does he like animals?" asked Tomas. "Dogs? Horses?"

Oh, now there was an utterly ballistic thought.

"Because one of our neighbors races malamutes and huskies, and he has been known to turn up dressed as Santa on Christmas Eve and take kids for a turn around the valley."

"Seriously?" Madeline couldn't think of anything more wonderful.

"Adults too, if you ask nicely," murmured Seth, and how could he read her so accurately. "Or you could go out to the Scott tree farm for a sleigh ride."

"Do they give sleigh rides after Christmas? My father and my brother and his fiancée won't be getting here until late afternoon on Christmas Eve."

"Worth an ask," he said.

"Fiancée?" echoed Savannah. "Your father is remarrying?"

Madeline nodded.

"What's she like?" asked the older woman.

"She's a surgeon." *Way to avoid the question, Madeline.* "And… I've never met her. Not that I haven't wanted to," she added hurriedly. "She's new." Oh, that sounded bad. "What I mean to say is that it was a whirlwind romance and I'll be meeting her soon. And I don't know my half-brother yet either but I hope to. Christmas is a good time for coming together, don't you think? There's like a… a format. I've been reading up on it. Practicing the food."

Savannah frowned. Everyone else looked on in silence. "I can cook." Was that why awkwardness ruled? "I just haven't Christmas cooked before."

"What do you usually do on Christmas Day?" asked Rowan quietly.

"Oh. I mean, there are all sorts of Christmas banquets to choose from in New York City." Even if the thought of going to one and sitting at a table by herself gave her chills. "I have a place in Midtown. I usually spend it there. But I haven't had Christmas with my father for a while, so I want everything to be wonderful this year. That's why Seth and his crew are working overtime to help me get the house ready." *Let's talk about that. Please, follow that conversational lead.* "I'm so happy with the work they've done so far."

And Rowan was nodding, and *please, please, someone pick up the conversation from there.*

"How long since you've had Christmas with your father?" asked Savannah. Leave it to a mother to zero in on the

KELLY HUNTER

weak spots in a story. She had five sons—she'd probably had way too much practice.

"Mom," Seth protested. "Stop grilling her."

"It's okay," she murmured. But it wasn't, really. It was mortifying. She didn't want to lie to these people who'd opened their home to her. "He's a very busy man." She dropped her gaze and reached for her knife and fork and cut into the tender, juicy turkey breast, adding a smear of cranberry sauce. "I was eleven last time I spent Christmas with my father. My mother was still alive and we were all together. It was perfect." Silence again and she couldn't stand the thought of them pitying her. "Which is why I am all on board with the thought of sled-dog rides and sleigh rides and a huge tree and all the snow and the magic of Christmas. I'm so looking forward to it."

"Sounds gorgeous," said Mardie, the lifesaver. "How can we help make that happen?"

Tomas picked up the conversation. "I can arrange for Jim Hicks to swing by on Christmas Eve with his sled dogs."

"Won't he be busy with his own family?" Madeline asked.

"He lives alone." Tomas shrugged. "He likes it that way."

Yes to normalizing people who were alone. Thank you, Tomas.

"And you don't need a tree from the tree farm," said Mason, looking toward Seth. "We'll come and cut one from your place." It was the most Seth's oldest brother had said all evening.

"Can it be a big one? Fifteen foot?" she asked. "It won't look out of place. The main living area is two stories high with an enormous stone fireplace and feature chimney running straight up to the roofline. Seth refused to board it up."

"I didn't refuse," he countered. "I put forward a rational suggestion that you use the fireplace a few times before you took that step. I wouldn't have said *no*."

"You threatened to weep!"

"You can't say that in front of my brothers!" He was playing along, moving the conversation away from absent fathers and into the realms of the ridiculous. "I have a reputation to protect! But, yes, to supersizing the tree. Come with us and choose it."

Yes. So much yes to the people in this valley. She wanted to repay them. She needed to repay them, and vowed that before she left this evening that the crate of wine would find its way to the doorstep whether Seth objected or not.

Conversation soon turned to securing a monster Christmas tree properly so that it wouldn't fall.

"I'm pretty sure you're doing me a favor with the tree," she whispered to Seth as others picked up different conversations around the table.

That whole section of conversation back there could have been labeled a help-Madeline session, but she didn't want him to think of her as a poor little rich girl starved for her father's attention, because she wasn't. She was moving away from being that person, finding strength and resilience that she never knew she had. "You can't spin it any other way."

"Not true." His low murmur rippled over her. "Something's up with Mason and he's never around enough to get him in a headlock and make him squeal. Give him a chainsaw and he turns into Mister Chatty. Trust me. We take him tree cutting and he'll spill his guts and thank us for the opportunity. We would be doing him a favor."

"I don't believe that for a hot minute."

"Maddie, I'm wounded. Why would I lie about a thing like that?" Smiling black eyes, gleaming with an invitation to play along.

"Is he going to yell his woes at us over the noise of the chainsaw? While one or both of you play lumberjacks?"

"Wash your mouth out. We don't play at being lumberjacks around here. When we cut forest trees we *are* lumberjacks. Born and bred."

It was the only part of this conversation she did believe.

"If your silent, brooding brother spills his guts during the Christmas tree acquisition process I'll…"

"Yes?" he inquired silkily.

"I'll give him a bottle of bourbon. The good stuff. And one for you too."

"Maddie, you hard-ass." How did his teasing always manage to make her feel so good? "That's just cruel."

WHEN JET AND Mardi made noises about heading home to Marietta so as to put their sleepy daughter to bed, Madeline glanced at Seth with a question in her eyes. He'd brought her, she had no other way of getting home and it was probably time she took her leave.

He nodded, and then there were thank-yous and good-byes and the rest of the wine to sneak onto the doorstep before they even got into his truck.

The drive home felt surreal after the warmth and noise of the Casey Thanksgiving feast. Seth didn't seem to feel the need for conversation, for one. A silver moon and a carpet of stars turned the snowscape otherworldly. New York City was never quiet the way it was here, even the sound of car doors opening and closing a subtle, muted click or thud.

"Can you hear it from here if there's an avalanche up in the mountains?" she asked idly, all full up on food and drowsily content.

"Not as a rule, they're too far away. No avalanche has ever reached your house, if that's what you're worried about."

"I wasn't. Was wondering about sounds. I hear elk some-times—I think it's elk, although I've never seen any. Maybe it's cows. I heard howling a couple of nights back, which I put down to wolves but it sounded a long way away. Can't say I miss the sound of sirens or garbage trucks, but it does sometimes feel as if I'm the only person on the earth."

"Does it bother you?"

"A little bit." It was easier to have such conversations with him when she didn't have to look at him and his attention was mainly for the road. She could take her time when it came to answering him. "I've lived alone since I finished school, so it's not that. Living alone out here's different."

She wasn't a hundred percent sure she liked it.

"Giving up already?"

"No, not giving up. I'm not putting the ranch on the market yet. Just getting smarter about what it means to live out here, I think. That's knowledge I didn't have until I got here."

"You're doing well," he murmured.

Before too long, they pulled up at her place and Seth cut the engine. She wondered if this was what it felt like to be sixteen and returning home from her first date with the cute guy she really liked checking out her parents' house to see if the coast was clear enough to steal a kiss.

The only glitch in her pretty-as-a-picture fantasy being that Seth knew full well no one else lived here and he didn't seem at all interested in leaning on over for that kiss.

She reached for the door handle.

Seth stopped her with a hand to her arm. "Wait."

"What?"

"Don't get out yet."

He still wasn't looking at her. Rather, he had his gaze trained on something to the left side of her house. She didn't like his stillness or the absolute focus with which he gazed into the distance. She hadn't liked the quick bark of his single word command.

"Stay in the truck," he said next, and when he used that voice she had no problem doing exactly as commanded. No problem at all. She leaned forward, following his gaze. "What do you see?"

Chapter Eleven

T O SCARE HER silly or not to scare her silly, that was the question.

But safety beat most other considerations. "Look over there."

She looked, she saw, she swore and grabbed his forearm in a vice-like grip.

"Is that a—" She left the rest of her sentence unfinished.

"Mountain lion. Cougar. Puma. Yes." Same thing. "It's really rare to see one up close. I haven't seen one in years."

"What do we do?" Panic laced her voice and lifted it an octave or two. "They didn't cover this at Swiss finishing school."

"You want to take a picture?" He took out his phone and did exactly that. "The first rule of telling tall tales to four brothers—pictures or it didn't happen."

Madeline still hadn't let go of his arm. He couldn't feel any tremors through the fabric of his coat but he did notice quite the white knuckled grip. He didn't want his valiant city girl giving up and returning to Manhattan with its blaring sirens and garbage trucks. He wanted to do everything in his power to help her tough it out.

"She's probably not used to seeing anyone around here and is as a surprised to see us as we are to see her."

"She?"

"Could be a he," he allowed. By and large, he thought cougars too pretty to be male and it showed in his terminology.

"Does anything in these mountains hunt cougars?"

"You mean apart from humans? No. They're apex predators. Are you sure you don't want to take a picture?" Her arm slid from his as he eased his driver's window down to take a few more shots, zooming in close. God bless fancy phones. "It's really rare for them to attack people."

"Couldn't you have led with that?"

"Sorry. You ready for me to make it go away?"

"How?"

He leaned on his car horn. Loud noises didn't always spook the big cats, but it was worth a try and this time it worked. They watched in silence as the big cat took off toward the tree line, slowing to a sinuous walk and looking back at them several times, its large eyes eerily reflecting the light from his headlights. "Guess you want me to walk you to your door."

"Good guess." She nodded vigorously. "And to come inside. And then I'm never letting you go. I have many bedrooms." She bit her lip. "I know I can't keep you, but I'd be forever grateful if you could come in and tell me what people do around here when the wildlife comes sniffing and what to look out for. How to live smart out here."

"I can do that."

He sent a quick picture of the cougar to Mason. It only took a moment for his brother to call him back. "You loaded?"

"Yeah." Had he said no, he knew without a doubt that Mason would have been up here handing over his best hunting rifle without question. Mason had gotten between him and a grizzly mama once, holding nothing but a slender tree branch and a burning will to protect.

Crazy older brothers.

"Call if you need anything," muttered Mason, and hung up.

"We won't have any trouble getting to your front door, but I'm going to get my rifle out just in case. It's with my tools in the back. You see anything move you lay on the horn, okay? I'll come round and open your door and then we'll head inside."

"Mountain man," she murmured.

Not even close. "More like valley born and bred. You'll get used to it." He wanted to believe that.

He got his gun and slipped a box of bullets into his coat pocket. He wanted the rifle for the scope more than anything else. He wanted to know where the mountain lion was headed.

The lights to the front door didn't come on as they approached, so that was the first thing they could set about changing. Maddie's bedroom had a patio entrance and the motion sensor lights weren't working there either. He ignored the clothes flung over the trunk at the end of her bed, but his gaze then went straight to her big king bed covered in every shade of blue he could imagine—he'd been in a woman's bedroom before, for heaven's sake, even if he'd never been in one that looked and felt so welcoming. That was Madeline's career description—to make rooms inviting. Didn't mean he'd come home.

"You've got all the gear," he told her as she hovered with her arms around her waist. "Outside light sensors and a sound alarm to wake you if anything happens by. Light and sound will warn most animals off and most importantly it will let you know if something's hanging around."

"I'm not sure letting me know about nearby mountain lions is such a positive."

She was trying to sound nonchalant, but her eyes held a lingering fear, even with him around. If she couldn't get a handle on her fears, she wasn't going to last out here alone. And while that could mean she'd sell and, more importantly, sell to him he had no intention of preying on her weaknesses.

"Cougars rarely attack people. They don't even come after our calves all that often. There's plenty of food for them in the mountains. This one probably got used to no one being here and now it knows you're here it'll carve your space out of its territory and be done with you."

"What about bears?"

"They're all asleep until spring but it's the same deal. Keep your household rubbish inside, don't compost, take your recycling into Marietta. And don't pee outside."

"I, ah, don't usually do that, no."

"Er, possibly a guy thing. Other guys, not me. Or my brothers." Five boys, two bathrooms. He felt his face redden. "We're housetrained."

"The Casey men have so many talents." She was smiling, at least. Willing to let her thoughts be drawn away from outside dangers.

"Turn the volume up on your favorite music. Make it obvious you're around."

"But didn't my turkey cooking bring the mountain lion here in the first place?"

"Maybe. But you can't tiptoe around out here. Gotta be present. Own it. Because you do."

"This isn't really a one-person place, is it?"

Nothing but the truth, even if it wasn't what she wanted to hear. "It's not for me to tell you what you're capable of. Only you can know that and oft times you never know until you try." There was that word again, the one he associated with her above all others.

Try.

He reset her outside light and went out to make sure it was working. "No prints on your patio," he offered when he returned and had closed the outside shutters and the big glass patio doors. "Snow makes prints easy to spot. Tomorrow morning we'll take a look around. Show you what the tracks look like, assuming it doesn't snow."

"Do I need to own a gun?"

He didn't know how to answer that for her. "If you do, you need to know how to use it. And when to use it."

She turned away, her shoulders slumped, and he wanted nothing more than to step up behind her, wrap his arms around her waist and let her lean on him while he comforted her. He could take her mind off mountain cats in the best possible way. Kissing would be involved, skin on skin and mind-stealing pleasure. His hands itched to reach for her.

"Got any hot chocolate?" he said instead. "Marietta has some really good chocolate shops."

"And I have discovered them," she replied with the tiniest of smiles. "Is it unreasonable to have an entire pantry shelf devoted to the stuff?"

"I like the way you think."

Which was how they ended up in her sunken lounge, mellow jazz music turned down low, hot chocolate in hand as his freshly set fire burned merrily in the grate. Maddie had browsed the upstairs library and returned triumphant with a book on big cats. She was currently tucked into one corner of the lounge with her boots off, hair down, and the book propped against her knees as she slowly turned the pages.

Guess he had a mountain lion to thank for his current level of lazy.

His mother's cooking. Sage's hot chocolate mix. Family. That woman over there. All of it had combined to make him fire-spelled and utterly content. "Tell me what you're thankful for," he murmured, and wondered if she'd reply. It wasn't a question for strangers, but he figured they were past that now.

She took a deep breath and sent her gaze skyward, toward the exposed beams of the ceiling way above them. "You mean apart from the Miss World obvious? Bette, my career mentor. I speak with her most every other day and she never says she doesn't have time for me. I invited her for Christmas and although she can't make it on the day she'll be here the day after. You'd like her, I think. Your mom would."

"What else?"

"This place," she offered quietly. "The opportunity to reconnect with my past rather than pretend it never happened. Even if living here does challenge my sense of self at every turn, I'm up for it. I want to grow." She reached over to the table for her hot chocolate and brought the mug to her lips. "I'm grateful I met you. You've been a huge influence on how easily I've settled here. You're generous when someone else would have walked away. You're kind."

He closed his eyes on her face lit by firelight. He wanted to be able to put that memory back together with his eyes closed. The glint of fire in the hair she'd so casually freed from her ponytail once they'd settled in for the night. Her slender sprawl and the stripy socks she'd added after she'd taken off her boots. The dangle of her earrings, the second pair he'd seen on her today—thin silver squares dangling inside one another, three of them, each a little smaller than the last, and the middle one all glittery with diamonds. They looked like they could have come straight out of some fancy modern art museum—all Picasso-ey and cubist and that was the sum total of his knowledge about art and he'd never been tempted to learn more.

There was something he wanted to get off his chest but he didn't know how to ease into it gently. An ugly rumor he was hearing more and more, and it concerned them both. "They're saying I'm after you because I want this place."

"I know."

So, she'd already heard it. Maybe from his crew who weren't above ribbing him about his attention to perfection when it came to the Love ranch renovations, maybe as early as that night at the saloon when she'd gone a little quiet on him and become more reserved when being introduced to people. He'd wondered. "They're wrong." He opened his eyes the better to gauge her reaction.

"I hope so." She'd abandoned the book and was eyeing him steadily, faint challenge in her gaze. "I know you're inviting me into your world. Allowing me access to your family. I know that means something and I'm grateful for the opportunity to see you more clearly. And for them—and you—to see me more clearly, hang-ups and all. I *want* to get to know you."

He could work with that. "Who's your favorite interior

decorator?"

"Dorothy Draper." Her eyes narrowed. "Do *you* have a favorite interior designer?"

"I curse them all." He watched her from beneath lowered lashes. "But I might look her up."

"Well, then." Her golden eyes were smiling. "I hope you like Hollywood Regency."

"Well, who wouldn't?" He'd made her smile. Best feeling in the world.

"If you liked the rustic mountain style of this place before I got my hands on it, *you* wouldn't," she informed him archly.

"I like what you've done with it." The floor rugs. The paintings on the walls and the furniture she'd shifted around until she had it exactly where she wanted it. Little bit of glitz and a splash of glam, bold color on the walls. "Did you know that the colors you choose make my painters phone in to see if anyone's made a mistake with the order when they first open the tin?"

"I suspected as much."

"By the time they'd finished they were all saying Seth, you gotta see this paint job. In a good way."

"Really?"

"Cross my heart."

She studied him for a moment, as if trying to divine the truth of his words, and then put her book down and left the sunken lounge area without a word.

He tried not to snag on the sway of her hips as she

climbed the half a dozen stairs and disappeared from view. He didn't watch and wait for her return either, but with it came a large hardback book titled *In The Pink* and, Lord help him, she handed it to him with a smirk and resumed her own reading.

Dorothy Draper had a lot to say about pink.

Could have been worse, he figured glumly as he stretched out along the lounge, a bunch of pillows at his head, and his feet up on a fluffy brown knee rug which meant that technically he didn't have his feet up on the furniture, and anyway, Madeline had her feet up too and that was good enough for him. Information meant growth and growth was good. This book was enormous. Who knew there was so much to learn...

About pink.

SETH CASEY WAS adorable when he was asleep. Madeline filed this information away for future daydreams. He had lashes to die for, thick and fanning out over bronzed skin. There was a hidden sweetness beneath his teasing that made her want to arch up into his hand like a little housecat, purringly content to be the center of attention. He made her feel safe. She was rapidly coming to the disconcerting conclusion that this house was never going to feel as good as it could feel unless he was in it.

When had she stopped designing this place as a show-piece for her skills and started thinking with him in mind? And herself in mind? And children?

They had a focus on family, these brand-new imaginary clients of hers.

They knew this land and its dangers, its beauty and its strengths. They wanted this home to be a place of rest, of nurturing love and vivid imagination, light and love and unending acceptance. These clients had nursery rooms and children's bedrooms picked out, even if they hadn't furnished them that way yet. There was a hand-made wooden cot in the basement. A painted rocking horse she remembered of old.

They were on her not-for-sale list. No way was she letting them go.

Slowly, she leaned forward and eased the book from his unprotesting hands and set it on the coffee table, standing it up so that the cover would be the first thing he saw when he awoke. She reached for a blanket, a pile of pink cashmere fluff, and draped it gently over his body. He made her smile, this man with no more favors to give. He'd seen her learning and trying to make sense of an unfamiliar word and responded by making a leap into his own unknown. Keeping her company, and not just in a physical sense.

With her heart full of something that felt a lot like tenderness, she added a couple more logs to the fire, turned off the lamplight and took herself to bed.

Chapter Twelve

ANOTHER WEEK WENT by, the first of December rolled around, and it was beginning to look a lot like Christmas in nearby Marietta. The shopkeepers had gone all out with their window decorations and strings of Christmas lights that decorated doorways and shop facades. Sparkly decorative snowflakes promised a glowing wonderland once the sun went down and community posters promised a Christmas Stroll to remember; an evening where the shops stayed open late and sidewalk musicians played festive tunes and carolers sang about holy nights and the hot chocolate and cookies and candy canes would be free for all and Santa would, of course, put in an appearance.

She marked it on her calendar and hoped the weather would cooperate. Driving around on regularly plowed highways wasn't hard so much as exacting. Living in the valley required consistent dedication to checking the weather report. Being sensible kept her safe.

Oftentimes, Savannah Casey turned up on a skimobile on the pretext of having just baked extra bread, or extra brownies, or cooked too much pie, but she always arrived just prior to extreme weather, and she always made a point of mentioning that it would soon be good weather for staying in.

"Do your sons *know* you snowmobile over to see me?" Madeline asked one day when it seemed to her that Savannah should definitely have taken her own advice and *stayed the hell inside*. "I know what you're doing. Honestly, next time you want me to stay put, just *phone* me."

But she couldn't deny that beneath Savannah's expert tutelage she also learned how to cook a turkey in the old wood fired oven, learned how to set a fire that would start with a single match, learned how to put certain sections of her too-large home into light hibernation so that the heating costs wouldn't cripple her.

Seth took to calling in most afternoons, usually on the pretext of checking on the work his crew had done that day. He often got on the tools himself in order to finish the work to his satisfaction—such a *perfectionist*—and if some evenings ended with drinks at the bar and dinner and conversation that ran late into the night, she wasn't complaining. She might even have wished for an unexpected snowstorm to strand him there on occasion, but the weather hadn't yet cooperated.

In the second week of December, Seth and Mason turned up on snowmobiles and took her out to the farthest corner of her ranch to choose a Christmas tree. They'd woven in and out of a stand of young trees until she tapped

Seth on the shoulder and pointed, and then her very own pair of lumberjacks had set to work, Mason not saying more than two words the entire time, and why would he? Her bourbon was in no danger whatsoever of leaving her possession, and they were undeniably doing her a favor as they roped the tree to the back of Mason's skimobile and dragged it carefully back to the house.

Getting it inside was a whole other production that required it first to be left in the barn so the snow on it could melt, before dragging it and the tarp it was on back up to the house and hauling it inside.

"Tell me again why the tree needed to be this size," muttered Mason as he and Seth strained to drag it through the foyer and into the main room. "How are you even going to reach the higher branches to decorate it?"

And then they got the tree to roughly where she wanted it and Mason stood up, looked around, and said, "Huh. I get it."

Even as Seth said, "Ladders."

Because the tree wasn't too big, it was perfect, and redolent with the sweet, refreshing scent of pine.

By the time they'd lashed it to the frame Seth had made for it, and stood it up, another hour or so had passed and they'd well and truly moved out of favor territory and into loud and completely ignored declarations along the lines of, *I really want to pay you for your time.*

And then Mason had noticed her snow shovel and

looked from her to the garage and from the garage to the barn and back to the house—and the triangular path between them all—and asked why she didn't have a snowblower, and *omg, snowblowers were a thing* and *why hadn't she ever heard of them?*

Taciturn Mason had a nice laugh and a surprisingly wicked smile when she turned on Seth and railed on him for not mentioning the possibility of having a snowblower in her life earlier.

Seth, who'd been stunned silent upon learning that she didn't already *have* one and had been shoveling all her pathways by hand.

Mason had laughed even harder at Seth's speedy apology and somehow the three of them had ended up in the downstairs bar, with Pappy for Mason and Wild Turkey for Seth because Seth was in the doghouse.

Talk turned to food and travel and somehow—with Pappy and Wild Turkeys involved—Mason revealed that he wanted to see Italy one day and swap snow for sunshine and BBQ ribs for spaghetti and pizza, at which point Madeline waxed lyrical for a while about her favorite Hell's Kitchen Italian restaurant and then went out on a limb.

"My new friend Cara, who's been staying at the Graff, petitioned the chef there for the use of his kitchen the other afternoon. She made us spaghetti alla puttanesca from scratch, and it was *amazing*. And then the chef told her it was a peasant's dish so she offered him a bite and now he's putting it on next Tuesday night's specials menu. A little taste of Italy right here at home if you're interested."

But Mason shut down fast and took his leave without responding to her suggestion at all.

"I guess I have a lot to learn about subtlety, don't I?" she said to Seth once Mason had disappeared. "I know they know each other. I know something happened between them. And I don't know if you or your brother know, but a lot of people around here are mean to Cara. Her money doesn't spend. Politeness gets her nowhere. She doesn't seem to have many friends, but I really like her."

Seth scrubbed at his jaw but otherwise stayed silent.

"Do *you* like her?" Seth's opinion was becoming increasingly important to her.

"I did when I was a kid." He picked up a coaster and started turning it with one hand. "Cara was dirt poor, scrappy, and thought Mason walked on water. Mason hung around with her when he thought no one else was watching."

"Classy." Not.

"Mason can be a dick. Status matters to him. It always has."

"And I guess it doesn't help that he has three very successful younger brothers."

"Yeah, well that's on him," muttered Seth with absolutely no give in him.

"What happened between her and Mason?"

"I don't know. Cara lit out of town the minute school

finished. Three months later she married a Texas billionaire old enough to be her granddaddy. No kids, he's now dead, Cara's back in Marietta, and Mason's…" Seth waved his hand in the direction of the door. "Struggling. Mason doesn't talk about Cara. He never has. He's not the one stirring up trouble for her."

"But people think she's a gold digger?"

"That about sums it up, yeah."

Madeline knew plenty of people who prioritized money over everything else. Her father was a prime example. But Cara didn't seem that far gone. Cara had returned home *knowing* what people would say about her and was reaching out in friendship regardless. That took courage. "It was really good spaghetti," she murmured wistfully.

"Next time… save me some."

THE NEW PICTURE windows arrived at the end of the second week of December and Madeline retreated to the Graff for three days while Seth and his crew installed them.

She didn't think the blindfold Seth made her wear was entirely necessary but stood patiently while he tied it, secretly delighting in his nearness and the awkward way he rearranged her hair once one of her mother's silk scarves was in place. It felt right to have some of her mother's possessions in use and scattered casually about the place. It felt equally rewarding to be putting her own stamp on the house, blending old with new, playing around with form and function.

Replacing the small row of windows with floor-to-ceiling sheets of reinforced, triple glazed glass had been her most expensive change to date. Instinct, her interior design education, and all the experience she'd gleaned from Bette made her confident about her decision, but thinking she was right was different to knowing she was.

Seth's hands felt warm on her shoulders as he guided her into the room and positioned her just so. "Ready?" he murmured and sent a delicious shiver down her spine as his breath teased her ear.

"I am." All of a sudden the blindfold made sense, the removal and now the return of her sight making her relish the moment.

She raised her hands to her face and slid the blindfold up and off. "Oh, my goodness!" The end result was better than she'd ever imagined. Her main room was now bathed in light, airy and open and that view—she took no credit for the valley and the mountains in the distance, but that view was impossibly beautiful.

"What do you think?" asked Seth, standing back and letting her take it all in.

"I love it. I can't believe you were against this to begin with."

"I wasn't *against* it. I had cost reservations. Gotta hand it to you though, Maddie, it's money well spent. There'll be no prying this place out of your hands now."

He looked so proud of his work and a little bit wistful at the same time. It was a look she hadn't seen on him before and she wasn't sure she liked it. "Did you know Cara's looking to buy a ranch around here?"

He nodded.

"She asked about this place and I told her you have first dibs on it, no matter what. I told my lawyer the same thing so that if ever something happens to me you've got it in writing."

This didn't seem to make him any happier. His mouth tightened to a thin, straight line and his dark eyes flashed a warning. "Nothing's going to happen to you. Don't say that."

"I thought you'd be pleased." *She'd* been pleased by the straightening of her business affairs.

"I am pleased, but you're making me getting my hands on this place sound like a consolation prize when you die, and I'd sure rather have you *present*."

How had they gone from window ogling to argument in the space of so few seconds? And how did she reply to the thought that he could actually, legitimately, want her to be present? "Can I hug you now, grumpy?"

"Might help."

Did help, as his arms came around her, and they stood looking at the magic he'd wrought on her home. "Thank you so much for pulling your crew off other jobs in order to get these in quickly. I heard the talk."

His people weren't exactly close-lipped. His crew liked to tease their boss man whether he was there or not, and she'd known before the windows even arrived on site that he had his best people all lined up and ready to go. "You put your best on this job, and yes, I do consider it a favor. Deal with it."

"They're all fired for blabbing." But she knew he wouldn't do that, and his wry smile confirmed it. "You're welcome. But I'm still charging you through the nose for it."

MADELINE HAD NEVER been happier than she was in the lead up to Christmas. She gift shopped. She fussed over her house furnishings, striving for interior design perfection, some kind of instantly recognizable aesthetic that would draw people in. With her creativity in full flow, Bette pulled her in on a high-profile New York loft apartment redesign and Madeline pounced on it like a starving bobcat—she'd been reading up on all the mountain cats—and turned a boldly masculine design around in record time. Could be she'd found it easy to meet that particular client's needs on account of all her recent exposure to masculinity and physically active ways of life. Could be her imagination now had room to soar, surrounded as it was by wide-open spaces and the beauty of nature.

Bette promised to arrive the day after Christmas and stay until New Year. Madeline put together a fabulously over-the-top bedroom for her treasured mentor, full of furnishings and fabrics she knew Bette would love. She intended to get Bette to choose anything she liked from the room as a Christmas gift.

She spent a lot of time putting together a couple of bedrooms for male guests, using some of the craftsman pieces she'd found in the basement. More wood, saturated blues and cloudy gray for the bedding. Deep club chairs in brown leather. An early renaissance biblical scene, suspected of being painted by the hand of a Venetian master. Madeline was a believer, even if no one could ever prove it. Every day, she learned more about her mother and her grandparents and every day she gave thanks for the opportunity and her growing sense of belonging.

She never did get around to putting a false floor over the sunken lounge area. It was Seth's favorite part of the house and when she bought a curved television screen and asked for it to be mounted on the wall down there it was worth it just to see the look on his face when he switched that thing on and found a ball game to watch.

The man was a comfort hound, but his lifestyle was very simple. Work. Warmth. Shelter. Food. And family and friends were somewhere in there too. She wanted to consider him a friend and maybe something more, but he hadn't kissed her again the way he'd kissed her that day at the bar and she didn't know why and hadn't gathered enough courage to ask him why not. She wasn't *needy* or *clingy*, or fragile or broken.

She was Madeline Love, talented and confident and *loving* every bit of every day leading up to Christmas.

She hoped her father would like what he saw—and that included the new, improved her.

December the twenty-fourth came with the promise of clear skies in the morning, with snow clouds closing in by late afternoon. They were predicting snow overnight but not feet of the stuff. Madeline's relationship with snow was complicated these days. Inevitably picturesque, it required hard work on a daily basis in order to just get around outside or travel into town.

Maybe one day she'd get a snowmobile and learn how to ride it through wind and snow like Savannah. Or maybe she'd wait a few years before fully embracing her inner mountain woman.

When her phone rang midmorning and she glanced at the caller name, she picked up with a smile.

"Symonds! Merry Christmas Eve to you."

"And you, Miss Madeline. How's Montana treating you?"

"It's cradling me in its arms like a beloved baby," she told him and meant every word. "Is my father on his way?"

Symonds paused. Madeline's entire body flooded with

that old familiar feeling as she leaned back against the kitchen counter and braced for the worst.

"It's the weather here."

"What weather? I checked the forecast for New York City an hour ago. What's wrong with the weather?"

"They're saying flights are likely to be delayed."

But she'd checked those too, an hour ago, and they'd been running on time. "They're not coming, are they?"

"Madeline, your father is a very busy man and what with the weather closing in, and flights to Bozeman potentially delayed, they reasoned—"

"Symonds, stop. Please, just stop with the excuses." She took a deep breath and reached calm. "Is my father there? Can you put him on the phone?"

"I can certainly try. He's looking at flight options as we speak."

They could still make this work. At least he was trying. "Is he trying to make it into Billings or Bozeman?"

"Neither."

"Glacier Park?" It was a long shot, a long way away from the ranch but they could make it work.

"Hawaii." Symonds's voice was laced with pity. "Young master Cade has decided he'd like to go to the beach."

There was no describing the desolation that ripped through her at those words. Her father's last-minute change of plans showed no consideration for her whatsoever. How much more proof did she need before she realized that she wasn't and would never be part of her father's new life?

All her preparation, all the trips and experiences she had planned for them, they didn't want them. They didn't want anything she had to offer.

"Madeline?" Symonds's voice had never sounded gentler. "I'm sorry. You know what he's like."

"Yeah, I know. I just… I was hoping for a new beginning, you know?" She took another deep shuddering breath, determined to get past this and finally move *on*. "Merry Christmas, Symonds."

"Merry Christmas, Miss Madeline. I may not be able to get the presents I have here for you to you before tomorrow, but I'll try."

She didn't want presents. "Don't worry about it. Please, it's Christmas Eve. Don't worry about them. Because I think—no, I know–that when it comes to trying to get my father's attention, I'm done." She walked through into the living room and looked around her beautiful home all dressed up for Christmas, with a tree that sparkled and glowed with old family baubles and new decorations she'd collected this year. She hadn't decorated that tree for her father—oh, it might have started out that way, but she'd found so much joy along the way, no need to be so sad. "I've finally had enough."

"You're not alone. Your father and I have been through a lot together, but today is my last day of employment here."

"But, Symonds, why? Are you ill? Why didn't you tell

me?"

"No, nothing like that. But I can no longer, in good conscience, bring myself to work for a man I've lost all respect for."

"But what's he done? Should I be worried about him?"

"No, young Madeline. There's nothing physically wrong with him and it's not as if he'd notice your concern. He's done wrong by you. It's your final straw, you say. Turns out it's mine as well."

All these years her father's executive assistant had been her point of contact when it came to accessing her father. *He'd* been the one to shepherd her through her school years. Making sure she had the right clothes at the right time. Passports, travel tickets, contacts. He'd been the one to introduce her to Bette. He was her partner in crime when it came to online antique shopping.

He didn't have family as far as she knew. He'd been dedicated to his work.

"Would you like to keep in touch with me?" she mumbled and felt the echo of those words deep in her soul. She'd asked exactly the same question on her first day of boarding school. Same words. Same man. "Because you want to, this time. Not because you have to."

"It would be my pleasure, Miss Madeline."

One day, she might even get him to drop the miss in front of her name.

"There's always Christmas in Montana to put on your

to-do list," she offered. "I have a lot of spare bedrooms and antique furniture to ogle. It's a great place for kicking back and taking stock of your life and refreshing your soul. Do I sound like a tourist brochure? I do, don't I? You're always welcome. And if you can't get to Montana, maybe we can do lunch when I get back to New York."

"Of course we can. Take care, Miss Madeline. I have to go."

Madeline began pacing after they ended the call. She took big breaths and blew them out as if she was a weight lifter working out with an eye to the Olympics. Huff and puff, huff and puff as she willed hot tears not to fall.

She'd had everything planned. Lighting up her Christmas tree for the very first time, sled dog rides courtesy of the lovely Jim and Casey family connections. She had gifts for everyone, gaily wrapped and bundled beneath the tree. She had enough food to feed a football team. Seth would be here any minute, calling in before heading off to host Casey Construction Company's Christmas party—maybe she could offload some of the food onto him. No point letting it go to waste.

She could do Christmas alone. How many times had she done it before?

Madeline and rejection were very old friends.

She could do this.

Seth came in after lunch, snow dusting his raven hair and the tips of an armful of old-fashioned roses. He had an enormous Christmas wreath in his other hand and a smile that had grown all too familiar. "Is this your new career?" she asked as she reached out to relieve him of the roses.

"I ran into Max from the florist and said I'd deliver these for him in exchange for a bunch of flowers for Mom. Christmas shopping is a nightmare."

"And you started your Christmas shopping when?"

He glanced at his watch. "Half an hour ago."

She'd started hers over a month ago. Not that the main people she'd shopped for were going to open her carefully chosen gifts tomorrow morning.

Seth took a good, long look at her and maybe she wasn't as adept at hiding her misery as she thought she was, but the next thing he said was, "What's wrong?"

She thought about giving him a nothing answer for all of five seconds, but he'd realize her father was a no-show soon enough when no one came into the valley on their way to her ranch and no one came out.

"They're not coming—my father and his fiancée and his son. And I'm not upset. It was always a long shot. He's a very busy man." Her voice broke on those very last words, and then she found herself chest to chest with him and encircled by flowers and strong warm arms.

"Your father's a fool."

"I don't think I can do this."

"Hug me? Of course you can. You're already doing it."

She burrowed harder into his warmth, borrowing strength, trying not to crush the roses.

"Have Christmas by myself here. I don't want to be alone. At least in New York I can be surrounded by other lonely people and we can be alone together. I can go see a show. The guys at the deli know my name."

"You're not selling me on a New York Christmas any time soon. Besides, I know your name. Lots of people around here know your name."

"Yeah, the Love heiress. The one you want to marry so as to get your hands on this place. People think I don't have ears."

"*People* are wrong."

"You can have it, you know. Make me an offer and I'll sell it to you."

"You don't mean that." He drew away, one arm still around her shoulders as he hung the Christmas wreath haphazardly on the hook she'd prepared for it. "Look at all the work you've put into it. You're just having a pity party is all. A well-deserved one because you were looking forward to showering your guests with a whole lot of love and now you can't."

He herded her into the house. "I have to go to the saloon and meet my employees. Everyone's off work now until after the New Year and today's the day I give out Christmas bouses. It doesn't last long, but it's a workplace tradition and the drinks are on me."

"I know. You already told me."

"I could come back later though, if you want some company. I know *I'd* like some company."

She was terrified she might be misreading him. "Only if you want to. Because it would gut me if this is you feeling all sorry for me and doing me a favor."

"I want to."

He took the roses from her unresisting hands and set them on a nearby table.

He framed her face with his hands—calloused palms and a gentle touch—and she closed her eyes as he dragged the pad of his thumb across her lower lip. And then he kissed her the way he had before; an irresistible mix of tenderness and passion and the undeniable ability to make all her troubles melt away.

"You could stay the night," she whispered, as he pulled her body flush against his, leaving no room whatsoever to doubt the strength of his arousal. "I have a lot of bedrooms. Including mine. Have you seen mine?"

"I could stand to see it again. And again. Though I should probably warn you that I'm not a one-night stand kind of guy. If we do this, tomorrow when we wake up all boneless and sated, I'll be reaching for you again. I'll be claiming a relationship with you. Is that what you want?"

"Yes." It came out a little breathy, probably on account of the kisses. "*Yes.*"

"I'll be back." He pulled away reluctantly.

"I'll be here."

Chapter Thirteen

WHEN MADELINE'S DOORBELL rang a little over an hour later, she figured it was probably Jim Hicks with his sled dog team. She'd been trying to get hold of him to tell him not to come but too late now. Maybe she could wow the man with a stint in the bar and beg his forgiveness before sending him on his way.

But it wasn't a grizzled mushing man, because there on her front porch stood Bette, a picture of glamor in a trouser suit, black boots, black coat, and beehive auburn hair. Beside her stood Cara, a vision of loveliness in this season's Burberry plum coat, skinny black trousers, and a silver-tipped fur scarf with hood.

"Bette!" She wanted a mom hug and got her wish. When had she grown so fond of hugging? Give her another Montana winter and she'd be downright touchy-feely. "Cara! Come in, come in. I have food." So much food. She couldn't wait for them to see the tree. "Bette, I wasn't expecting you for a couple more days! How did you get here?"

"Madeline, my sweet, that's a story I need to tell you over wine."

"Come through. I have wine." So much wine. "What would you like?"

"Pino grigio, dar—oh, my *Lord*." Bette had entered the main room her gaze at first drawn to the bank of windows and then the rest. "Your pictures don't do it justice."

"Told you," murmured Cara who'd been out here a week or so ago. "By the way, Madeline, I am so sorry to gate-crash your family get together on Christmas Eve, but I met Bette in the hotel foyer—"

"And there are no rooms left at that particular inn," muttered Bette. "My flights for the twenty-sixth got canceled this morning, and they offered me flights for today instead so I took them. The weather in New York was turning mean anyway. I got to Bozeman no problem, and from there I caught a lift to Marietta with a lovely couple I met on the plane. They dropped me at the hotel, which is fully booked—I should have known better than to trust that online booking site, and that's where I met Cara who very generously offered to drive me here. In my defense, I didn't know what I was asking of her. Thank heaven she knew the way. It's snowing out there!"

"Only lightly," said Cara. "I'll get back okay."

"Or you could stay. Why not, if you can swing it? I have many spare bedrooms, and my father has canceled so it's just me." Bette looked wholly unsurprised. "And maybe Seth a bit later." Would he still want to stay once he realized she had unexpected guests? "And I'm expecting a neighbor to drop by with his sled dog team—it was a surprise for my little brother, but everyone likes sled dog rides, right? Bette, you could try?"

Bette's eyes narrowed thoughtfully. "I always could picture myself tearing through the snow yelling *mush*."

"How about I get you both settled in bedrooms upstairs and then you can join me downstairs in the legendary Love ranch bar for some finger food and whatever you feel like to drink, and we'll take it from there."

Cara looked torn. "I don't have an overnight bag with me. I feel bad for imposing. Also, you have Caseys."

"Only the one Casey and he has nothing but good to say about you. I have guest toiletries by the boxload. And you can have at my wardrobe if you need clothes." Perhaps she could persuade Cara to stay for Christmas lunch. "But I understand if you have other people to see. It's Christmas Eve." Of course Cara would have somewhere else to be. "Unless you're like me and Bette and your plans have fallen through?"

"I don't have anywhere else to be," Cara said with quiet dignity, and boy was Madeline well acquainted with that feeling.

"Sooo, let me practice my hospitality on you. You'll be my first guests. It's bound to be a disaster. You'll be doing me a *favor* by staying." Madeline had definitely been hanging around Seth for too long and learning many bad habits.

"I'm sold," said Bette. "Bring on the catastrophe."

"Cara?"

"Okay."

Yes! The day was looking up. "Honored guests, welcome to my not so humble, dressed for show abode. Let me show you to your rooms."

Chapter Fourteen

F OR THE FIRST time in his life, Seth wanted his crew to drink fast, take their bonuses, and leave. Normally, he would take the time to find out who was traveling or going on vacation over the break, he'd listen up and find out what was happening in people's home lives, make a note of due dates if there were any babies on the way, or upcoming weddings. Connecting with people. This time he left all that mainly to Jett while he brooded over whether he was taking advantage of Madeline's disappointment and loneliness and inserting himself into the picture like an opportunist.

"Hey," said his brother. "You still with us?"

"Yeah." He picked up his beer, only to pause when it came to putting it to his lips. He'd been sitting on it all afternoon and it was flat and warm.

Jett sighed heavily and signaled for another. "I suppose you're going to sit on that one too?"

"Probably."

"The guys are happy with their bonuses. They're calling it the Love Bomb Bonus. Chalking it up to your soon-to-be partnership with the heiress. They can't decide if you're going to go into business with her and harness her interior design skills or marry her and become a cattle rancher. You might want to hose those rumors down."

Trouble was, he didn't know what to replace them with.

He was tired of trying to bury his protective instincts around Madeline. Of making up excuses to be with her. He was getting sick of shoveling a mountain of bull about doing favors for other people that also happened to benefit her. Why *couldn't* he make her life easier if he wanted to? Why did he need to hide his desire to?

He was so *over* his stupid one-favor rule.

"She's the one." It felt good to finally get that out in the open, even if Jett had that look about him that said Seth was telling him nothing new. "I wasn't looking for the one but there she is, and I hate that people think I'd put land before love. What do they take me for? Can't they *see* her? She could have nothing but the shirt on her back and a man would still be lucky to have her."

"Don't tell me." Jett looked uncommonly embarrassed. "Tell her."

"I plan to." Although it wouldn't hurt to make sure everyone else knew his position on the matter, starting with this crew right here. They could then indulge their blackened, gossiping souls and spread the word. What else had Jett said? Time to hose those rumors down.

He set his beer back on the table and stood. "All right, listen up." Authority sat well on him. He'd worked his way to the top of this particular pile, and he was ambitious and opportunistic, but only in a business sense. Not with his heart. That was his to guard and more importantly, his to give. "We've had a good year here at Casey Constructions, and we have another big one lined up. I want to thank you all for being part of that. I want to thank you for working harder, and smarter, and putting in the extra time in the lead up to Christmas so I could fit in another job. You know the one I'm talking about. Even though the Love ranch isn't mine, it was a project of the heart for me and the results are outstanding. You should be proud of that. I'm proud of it."

Give 'em praise before criticism and then praise again afterward. That was the plan.

"I also know you're a bunch of gossipy old windbags and that your speculations about my private life are starting to hurt people. You call a woman who treats every one of you with respect *the Heiress*—as if that's all she is. You imply there's no other reason for my interest in her other than to get my hands on ranch land I've always wanted. That's a rumor that needs to stop. It's not true. It disrespects us both."

He had their attention now, damn sure he did. Go big or go home. He'd started his business with exactly that attitude. It seemed only fitting that he signal his intentions toward Madeline in much the same way. "I am in love with Madeline Love. All the way gone, there's no going back, and I will cut out my heart before I hurt her. If any of you hurt her, I'll cut out yours, too."

He didn't expect the whooping and hollering that erupted at the end of his warning speech. The giant smiles and the bellows of laughter. The thumps on the back and the *I'm happy for you, man*s.

He probably should have expected the betting on his love life and the money currently changing hands.

"So, are you bringing her to Mom's for Christmas?" asked Jett, after he'd collected his winnings with a smug grin.

And he could do that. Railroad her in much the same way he'd secured her presence at his mom's table for Thanksgiving. Her father wasn't going to be there and it'd be better than her spending Christmas alone. But then he remembered all the practice cooking she'd done, and the relentless work she'd put into getting the ranch house glowing like a treasured jewel. How she'd poured so much of her heart into the decorations. "Nah. I might take a pass on Christmas at Mom's this year and spend it with Maddie instead." If she'd have him. "She's pretty cut up about her dad and his new family changing their plans at the last minute, and she's done all the prep."

Jett's eyebrows rose. "That's not going to go down well with Mom. You not being there."

"She likes Madeline."

"Uh-huh. Maybe you should aim to keep it that way."

"I can still call in for a bit. Mom will understand."

Jett looked down at the hefty pile of winnings in front of

him and then back up, a gleam of avarice in his eyes. "How much do you wanna bet?"

BETTE AND CARA settled into the ranch space with unabashed delight that warmed Madeline to the core. Bette had nothing but praise for the design magic she'd wrought, and Cara inflated her ego to bursting when she said, "Madeline, I feel like I've stepped into a Christmas card. It's so beautiful, but homey too, even with all the museum pieces and the super-luxe approach. How? How do you do that? And who's this gorgeous woman in this portrait?"

"That is Grandma, Peggy, the woman I have to thank for buying this ranch in the first place and making sure it passed down to my mother, and from there to me. Isn't she elegant?"

"And who's this woman in the next portrait? The one who looks even more like you."

"That's my mother, Elise."

"Stunning, isn't she?" said Bette, coming to stand beside Cara, wineglass in hand and a sheer silk nineteen seventies-style caftan replacing her earlier travel clothes. "I love where you've hung them. Right here in the heart of the home so they can see all the action."

"You need to get your portrait painted, too," declared Cara, and started off a round of no's from Madeline and

Bette when it came to what style of portrait to choose.

The sled dogs arrived under the command of rugged mountain man Jim who had a look of weathered Sean Connery about him, which entertained Bette to no end. She'd come for the cowboys, Bette told him, but he looked like he would do.

Weathered Jim wasn't backward about coming forward to claim cowboy status, too.

It took no persuasion at all for everyone to rug up and meet the dogs and take a turn on the sled, although Jim never gave up the reins. He did let Bette give the dogs all the verbal commands when it was her turn to go.

Wine had nothing to do with Madeline's laughter when the hillsides rang out with Bette's joyful, "Mush, Dancer. Mush, Prancer. Mush, Rudolph, *Muuuuuush up!*"

It was a wonder those *reindeer* didn't deliver her back to New York.

They took the party downstairs to the bar and Madeline laid out all the snacks she'd prepared for other guests who didn't know what they were missing and then she slipped behind the bar and listened to Jim tell tall tales about ski sled races across the mountains and finishing line parties held right here at the bar. His dogs were pegged out on the patio, resting lumps of fur waiting to make the trip home, and Madeline offered fat uncooked steaks for their dining pleasure. She did have enough to feed a football team, and she was all about not letting food go to waste, but Jim nixed that idea, although he thanked her for the offer. He'd run them hard and fast on the way home and he didn't want them doing so on a full stomach.

He didn't seem to mind so much when it came to lining his stomach with a glass or two of cognac. That was how Seth found them when he walked in, having let himself in the unlocked door when she'd failed to answer it, his expression so quizzical that she had to counter it with a hug before introducing Bette, who immediately launched into an embellished tale of how she'd gotten here.

He already knew Jim.

He already knew Cara.

And while Cara looked uneasy with the addition of Seth, he soon had her laughing at his story of a glass-domed yoga tower with glass defrosters built in and a fire pole exit right next to the slippery slide next to the stairs.

He and Bette bonded as they listed ever more ridiculous 'vision statements' they'd received from clients. Bette won that round, hands down, and Seth washed down his defeat with a laugh and a shot of bourbon.

When Jim made tracks and headed home, they made their way upstairs and Madeline took the opportunity to take Seth aside and introduce him to the guest suite opposite hers.

She'd designed the room with men in mind and it had something of a Knights of Old vibe about it. Bare wood floor liberally draped with deep pile deep-blue floor rugs occasionally connected by the presence of Persian carpets. Blue velvet curtains, midnight-sky bedding with icy-gray bedsheets and pillows. A rustic wooden king-sized bed, a leather club chair and side table over by the window, and the stone fireplace upgraded and set behind glass doors so as to meet fire regulations.

At the bottom of the bed sat a trunk full of blankets. One doorway led to a walk-in closet, the other door to a bathroom complete with a shower for two and huge tub for soaking in.

"I didn't know what you'd be thinking now that we have visitors," she began awkwardly, and winced at her liberal use of the word *we* to describe *her* unexpected guests. "My bedroom's the one opposite yours, and I've put Bette and Cara upstairs. Not that I expect you to sneak around, I just didn't know if their presence changed anything and I didn't want to presume."

"They have kind of foiled my seduction plans," he said, his eyes alight with laughter. "But I can improvise. Bette's a hoot."

"And Cara?"

"Your house, your guests. You like her. I have no quarrel with her, and as long as I don't go giving any of Mason's secrets away, I can probably still claim loyal brother status. I wouldn't necessarily invite her somewhere I knew Mason was going to be—not without fair warning—but that doesn't apply here."

It was enough. "How did your work party go?"

His face took on a pained expression. "Jett assures me it was memorable. One for the ages."

"Do tell?"

"Never, ever gonna tell, Maddie. What happens at the work Christmas party stays at the work Christmas party. It's the rule."

Curious. "Okay, so I'm just going to offer the ladies some pie and a nightcap or a hot chocolate and then I'll probably turn in. You're welcome to join us."

He shrugged. "Still working on my adjusted game plan here."

Hopefully, it would involve her finding him naked in her bed. The thought brought quick heat to her cheeks. The perils of being a redhead.

"I'll just leave you to settle in." She didn't want to leave him. "Let me know if there's anything you need."

"I will."

Madeline left and found Bette and Cara making themselves at home in the newly designed breakfast booth area of the kitchen with an open bottle of champagne between them and three full champagne glasses on the table.

"We helped ourselves," said Bette, which was exactly what she'd asked them to do. "We're waiting for Santa to come down that chimney. He'll probably bring Rudolf in, too. It's big enough."

Madeline loved her supersized heart of the home fireplace these days, thank you very much. To think she'd once been determined to board it up.

"Seth all sorted?" asked Bette archly.

"Yeah, I think he's thinking of turning in."

"Or not," murmured Cara as her gaze slid past them toward the open plan kitchen.

"Ladies." Seth was barefoot, his collared shirt untucked. The sleeves were rolled to his elbows and every single button on the front had somehow come undone to give a tantalizing glimpse of a set of six-pack abs and truly impressive chest. Swinging a hammer all day clearly came with benefits.

"Just coming to get a glass of water." He opened the door and leaned down to take a good long look before reaching out and snagging a bottle of the stuff that was exactly the same as the bottles of the stuff sitting on his bedside table and in his bathroom. "Thanks."

He sauntered away, seemingly undaunted by the silence he left in his wake.

"Invitation?" asked Cara and sipped her champagne.

"Absolutely an invitation," agreed Bette. "Madeline, honey, that little display was entirely for you—even if we did all benefit."

"I might need a little more courage." Madeline reached for her champagne.

"Not too much," advised Bette. "You have things to do."

Five minutes later, he was back.

Bare feet, low slung jeans and belt.

And no shirt at all.

"Can't find my phone," he said and made a bold show of looking for it, even going so far as to check Madeline's kitchen drawers. The lower ones, where she kept all the pots and pans.

"Poetry," said Bette. "Pure poetry. Have you tried the fridge? You might have dropped it in there last time you were here?"

So he looked in the fridge again too, leaning down, long of leg, such lovely muscled lines running through his shoulders, arms and back. Had she been Rembrandt, she'd have been telling him to twist, yes, just like that, and hold those grapes in his hand a little closer to his lips.

He stood back up, and one grape disappeared, plucked from the bunch by his strong white teeth as he boldly held her gaze.

Bette snorted. Cara choked on her champagne bubbles.

Madeline loved every outrageous moment. "Still no phone?"

"Must be somewhere else," he murmured once he'd swallowed his grape and they'd swallowed their tongues. "'Night, ladies. 'Night, Maddie."

Once again, he turned and headed for his room.

"Didn't you put a fruit basket in his room?" said Bette. "Mine has one."

"I didn't. But he does have the Titian masterpiece in his room. Plenty of bare chests there. Maybe it's giving him ideas."

"I think it's nice that he's making himself comfortable," murmured Cara. "Don't you, Bette?"

"Oh, I *do*."

"I know you're mocking me." Madeline felt obliged to comment. "Or him. Or something."

"But we're doing it with love," said Bette. "What's the bet we see more of him?"

"I'll take that bet," said Cara. "Looking forward to it."

"Remind me not to seat you next to each other at breakfast tomorrow. Better still, sleep in."

"Who sleeps in on Christmas Day? Anyone?"

"I'll take that bet," said Bette. "Madeline will."

"Not fair!" And then Cara looked past them again, a hedonistic smile blooming as she picked up her champagne glass and sent a silent toast skyward.

Madeline turned. Blinked. Never had her eyes felt so wide as Seth padded closer, naked as the day he was born but for a couple of glossy hardback coffee-table books held low to strategically hide his nether regions.

"Maddie, I need your help," he began. "I couldn't sleep so I figured I'd read for a while, but I don't know which one to choose. This one?" He held a Dorothy Draper picture book of the Greenbrier Hotel up to his chest. "Or this one?"

The other book was about interior designer David Hicks and those books changed places lightning fast, with the Hicks one heading chest-ward and the Draper book descending, quick as a flash, and she did cop a flash. The man was shameless.

But not as shameless as Bette.

"Hard to say," said the older woman. "Ask us again."

"No!" Had Madeline been ten, she would have kicked Bette beneath the table in an effort to make her behave. "Try the Hicks," she told him. "His style is very fresh."

"Thanks." Seth held her gaze, his eyes alight with the promise of very good times and a question only she could answer.

He turned, his very fine, very bare ass fully on show, and sauntered back to his room.

Silence reigned until Bette sighed with delight. "That was beautiful," she proclaimed. "Simply beautiful. Every home should have one."

Madeline drained her glass and stood. "Well, I don't know about you, but I'm for bed." Before Seth came up with any other ideas. "Merry Christmas, sweet dreams, I'll see you in the morning."

"Good for you," murmured Cara. "He's putting himself way out there just for you, and he's a keeper. Be good to him."

There was absolutely no pretending that she wasn't one hundred percent gone on the man. "I'll do my very best."

The last glimpse she had of her old mentor and new friend was of them clinking their glasses together, happily content.

Madeline retreated to her own room first, to freshen up

and change into something a little more comfortable.

That something comfortable was a baby-doll nightie made from white chiffon and lace. She took down her hair and brushed it out and then added quick waves with a styling brush. She touched up her makeup, not too much but enough to paint a pretty picture, because a show like the one Seth had just put on for her demanded a little effort in return.

Ten minutes later, she stood in front of Seth's door and knocked. The door opened immediately and there stood Seth, magnificent in his nakedness, not a coffee table book in sight.

"That was quite a show."

"Did you like it?"

"Loved it. It's what dreams are made of." Her dreams, at any rate. She wanted to turn her dreams into reality. "May I come in?"

He smiled and filled her heart. "I thought you'd never ask."

Chapter Fifteen

S ETH WOKE LATE. These things happened after a long night full of loving followed by falling asleep on a cloud. Sunlight filtered in through curtains they hadn't bothered closing, and the fire he'd lit last night had burned down to black coals. Not that he cared, he was plenty warm enough beneath the bedcovers and there was a sleeping woman at his side. One with auburn hair and skin so soft and pale he feared she'd bruise beneath his touch. But she'd proved herself resilient last night, her deeply giving nature a beloved gift he had no intention of giving up.

Madeline stirred, turning into him and snaking a warm arm across his stomach in a move he hoped to hell was possessive. She settled again with her head on his shoulder and flung a leg across him as well.

He wasn't complaining.

"That was some show you put on last night," she murmured sleepily and he felt his chest puff.

"Thank you. Thank you very much."

"Bette's going to want a repeat."

Oh, *that* show. "Had to get your attention somehow."

"It worked." She eased up onto her elbow, her gaze intent. "Pinch me."

And put a mark on that skin? "Not on your life."

"You're the best thing that's ever happened to me. How else am I going to know this is real?"

He had a few ideas.

"I mean it," she said. "No one's ever made me feel so good about just being me."

"Well, you see, mankind is stupid and I'm very willing to take advantage. I know a true heart when I see it."

"But you haven't seen my heart."

"Yeah, I have. And it's full of kindness and loyalty, honesty, and try. You never stop trying, never stop giving—it's what I love about you the most."

He watched his words hit and her momentary confusion. "You love me?"

"Too soon?"

"*No!*"

Fairly forceful that answer. Smile inducing.

"I mean, no," she continued with far more composure. "I could stand to hear that some more."

"Every day?"

"Definitely every day. Because I feel the same way."

He gathered her closer. "Want to join forces with me? What's yours can stay yours, including this place. I don't ever want you buying into the idea that I'm here for your belongings rather than for you."

She flopped back on her pillow and stared at the ceiling and it was his turn to prop himself up on an elbow the better to see her face.

"Want to do me a favor?" she said finally.

"Anything."

"Forget about what other people think and propose to me one day, whenever you're ready. I want to share all I have with you. I guarantee I'll say yes."

They were late for breakfast.

Chapter Sixteen

CHRISTMAS DAY FELT different this year. Full of promise and new beginnings. Ripe with Bette's fulsome praise for her interior design skills. Bubbling with Cara's dry wit and gratitude for including her—there were depths to Cara she hadn't yet navigated. Full of Seth, fully clothed again, praise be.

This home. This time and place. She'd never been so happy.

Everywhere she went was filled with love and she'd worked hard to make it that way and it was Christmas Day and she was *home* and the feeling of love was overwhelming.

And then the doorbell started ringing.

Mardie, Jett, and young Claire were the first to arrive, laden with gifts and food and Madeline had no idea what was going on, but she rolled with it, inviting them in, filing away their reactions to her home and her Christmas tree for future viewing.

Bette proved to be the social lubricant every function needed as Seth and Jett hunted down extra leaves for the Christmas table set split-bang alongside her new picture windows.

The turkey was in the oven and Cara was in command of the sides. The log fire was burning, and music was playing.

"What's happening?" she asked Mardie.

"Seth bailed on Christmas at Savannah's and that was not acceptable," Mardie said. "So we took a family vote and decided we'd have Christmas at your place this year. Seth doesn't know and I hope you don't mind. If it gets too much just give me a signal and I'll round everyone up and we'll leave."

"It won't get too much."

Mardie reached out for a hug. "Welcome to the family, Madeline."

Tomas and Rowan, baby Joseph James, and Rowan's father were the next to arrive, and it wasn't a problem because the table got extended again and she had more than enough tableware, even if it didn't match, and she had Bette, who assumed the role of a general who'd been waiting all her life to command such a laughing, free-wheeling willing army.

When the doorbell rang again and it was Mason, she stared at him in panic because she'd completely forgotten that Cara was still here and that Cara and Mason had history.

"Merry Christmas," he said quietly. "I hear this is the place to be."

"I—That is, Cara—"

"I know she's here. Seth texted me. I'm housebroken,

even if it sometimes seems otherwise. I won't make a scene."

"Come in," she said. "You're welcome. I'm so glad you're here. This is crazy. Your family is crazy." And brilliant along with it.

"Don't expect me to argue."

She closed the door behind him and followed him into the living room with its roaring fire and crazy sunken living room and huge dining table that hadn't yet run out of extension leaves, although she had needed to break out several different sets of glassware.

Her Christmas table was far from perfect, there hadn't been enough of any one type of silverware, any one type of plates or napkins or bowls and it was still the most perfect Christmas table she'd ever seen.

The floor beneath her Christmas tree was awash with gaily wrapped gifts and she didn't know how or when any of them had arrived or who they were all for or when they were going to start opening them.

She was winging it.

Loving every moment.

Savannah and Cal arrived, laden down like donkeys with even more food and Madeline could have sworn the house pulsed with warm welcome at their entrance.

Drinks flowed, laughter rang out, and Madeline couldn't help but find Seth among the throng because all she wanted to do was hug him. Even better when he lifted her off her feet and swung her around as if she weighed nothing.

"Next time we do this I think we should bring on the spit-roasted wildebeest," she told him.

"Whatever you want. I apologize. Gate-crashers, all of them."

"They love you. *I* love you. Now put me down. I can't believe the doorbell's ringing again. Maybe it's Jim with his sled dogs. Bette invited him."

But it wasn't Jim. Symonds stood at the door, a lean travel bag at his side and the biggest bunch of peonies she'd ever seen in his arms.

"Symonds?" She could hardly believe it.

"I couldn't get anyone to deliver your flowers at such late notice, so I decided to bring them myself."

He felt so stiff and upright beneath the weight of her sudden hug, but she dragged him in anyway and started introducing him around. He and Bette were old friends and soon enough he was enmeshed in the group and looking only slightly the worse for wear. She showed him to an upstairs room and found a vase for those beautiful flowers and put them on a sideboard in the main room where her mother and grandmother's portraits could see them.

She caught Seth's gaze and then found herself in his embrace again, flustered and incredulous and so damn happy she could burst. "That's Symonds, my father's former executive assistant. He noticed me. He held me up when I was a kid with nothing and no one. Be nice to him. I have plans for employing him if my interior design career ever gets off the ground."

"I will welcome him to the family."

"Look at us." Awe had set in alongside gratitude. "All of us. This house is so happy now. Look at it."

But he only had eyes for her, and that made her even happier.

How her modest turkey was supposed to feed everyone she didn't know, except that there was a honey-glazed ham to go in the electric oven and Mason and Cal were tossing foil-wrapped potatoes into the open fire and arguing over the merits of tossing a foil-wrapped side of spareribs on there too.

It was worth a try, she told them. Anything was possible. Madeline was a believer.

Mason and Cara hadn't spoken yet, but they had exchanged glances and a delicately flushed Cara had been the first to look away.

The food was almost ready to go on the table when the doorbell rang again.

Madeline groaned. The table now seated fifteen and there were only a couple of extension sleeves left. Maybe it was Jim.

But when Madeline opened the door Jim was nowhere in sight.

Instead, her father stood there, wearing a long overcoat and dark trousers, patent leather shoes, and an uncertain face. He had one hand on a young boy's shoulder and his other held tight in the grasp of a woman she didn't know.

"Madeline." His voice was low and measured. "We made it after all."

"Who is it?" Seth had snuck up behind her, and it seemed he was quicker than she was when it came to reading the room. "You must be Madeline's father," Seth said coolly, his black eyes pitiless. And then he noticed the boy. "And you must be Cade. Want to come and see our tree? Because I think I saw some presents underneath it with your name on them."

"I'll come too if you don't mind," said the woman with short dark hair and kind blue eyes and who looked nothing like her mother and yet Madeline just knew they would have inexplicably *got* one another. "I worked a double shift at the hospital yesterday and it's been a very long journey and I'll sing for a coffee. No, really, I will. My passion is amateur theater. Be very afraid."

Seth took it all in stride. Maybe that was what having four other brothers did for a man. "I'm Seth, come in. We don't have any singers here yet, so the stage is all yours. Know any carols?"

She loved that man, disappearing through the entrance vestibule with a young boy and tired surgeon in tow.

Leaving her and her father alone.

And she didn't want him in there in her happy place. It was still too new, too unbelievable, to withstand his calculating gaze. Call it self-preservation, call it way too many years' worth of needing answers from him and never getting them, but she would not let him spoil this Christmas for her.

She wrapped her arms around her middle, and it had nothing to do with the nip in the air. "Symonds said you weren't coming. Not that you had the grace to tell me yourself. What happened? Couldn't you get any last-minute tickets to Hawaii?"

His lips tightened as he met her gaze. He always had been a handsome man, her father, but he was getting older and the grooves in his face made him look drawn. He looked pale, but maybe that was because she'd grown used to the tans of the outdoorsmen all around her.

"No, I secured tickets for Hawaii. And then Symonds handed in his notice and my fiancée told me I wasn't the man she thought I was."

"Nothing to do with me, then." It figured. Always a fool for expecting anything different. "I don't know what to say to you anymore."

"Except that you sent me a Christmas message this morning and, even though it wasn't a video like I was used to, you said, *Merry Christmas, Dad. I love you and I hope that wherever you are you're happy.* And it showed me that your capacity for love and forgiveness is nothing short of a miracle, and I wondered whether you might be able to forgive me for leaving you and your mother here all those years ago. For leaving her to die and you to watch. For making a child do what I couldn't. I'm so ashamed. I can't forgive myself for my actions. I never will, and you look so much like her, and you love like her too. Completely, whether someone deserves it or not."

"Why are you here? I was ready to let you go. I really was." And now he was here, and she couldn't do it.

He was her father.

The memories welled up out of nowhere and wouldn't go away.

She was an airplane and his strong arms were the only things holding her up.

She was on a toboggan, sitting in her father's lap as they sped down a snowy hill.

She stood on his shoulders, a white and gold porcelain angel in her hand as she placed it ever so carefully at the very top of the Christmas tree, and her mother was there, looking on with such *love*.

Not just a surname.

A choice.

To love and to forgive.

To start over, from this moment forward, but only if he was willing to grow too. "You asked me to remove all traces of Mom from this house, but I haven't and I never will. She's in the furnishings and the decorations on the tree and the portrait on the wall and I won't let you take her away from me. So, if you can't deal with that maybe you should gather up your other family and keep right on driving."

Would he do it? She braced herself for rejection and felt

her mother's spirit in that moment, giving her strength. His loss, not hers. It was the right decision. "I'll let you think on it a while and if you do decide to come in, well, I haven't changed the place that much. You know your way around."

SHE LEFT HIM outside with the stars and his heart for a compass and made her way back into the warmth. She met Seth's questioning gaze and shrugged, and he was by her side moments later, one arm around her waist as he danced her to the windows and then slowed to a shuffle, seemingly in no hurry to let her go anytime soon. He studied her intently, his body warm and hard against hers.

"Do I need to make your father wish he was never born?" he murmured. "Because, believe me, all you need to do is nod."

"You'd do that on my nod?"

"In a heartbeat. I'm done with pretending I don't want to protect you, that I don't want to favor you a dozen times a day."

"You really weren't doing a good job of pretending indifference," she said and pressed a gentle kiss to his cheek, mainly because if she aimed for his lips, she'd get lost in him and there were others to consider. "Let's wait a bit. My father might join us, he might not. What's his fiancée like?"

"Rebecca? So far so good. She seems like a woman who

knows what makes people tick and who doesn't shy away from difficult situations."

"And Cade?" Her little half-brother she'd only glimpsed in passing. He had a shock of dark hair and a pale complexion. Light blue eyes, like her father. Their father.

"Quiet. Wary. He keeps looking toward the entrance. He refused a drink, but he did it politely."

Madeline looked over Seth's shoulder and spotted the boy kneeling to one side of the tree but making no move to look at the presents. Instead, Claire was talking at him ten to the dozen, with a plastic pony in each hand—one yellow with a pink mane and one purple. She watched as he pointed to the yellow one, which Claire promptly handed to him. He turned the plastic toy over in his hands and then won Madeline over by offering a timid smile and then galloping the toy across the floor to nibble at Claire's shoes. "I should go and say hello."

She squeezed Seth tight and then pulled away and walked toward the tree and the little crowd who had gathered nearby.

She smiled at Rebecca who'd just accepted a coffee mug from Bette. Madeline let her be and hoped the other woman would understand her current priority.

She went up to the children and sat on the floor, surprised and grateful when Claire with her pigtails and Christmassy hair bows—one red and one green—plopped down in her lap and continued to play ponies with Cade.

"Hi, I'm Madeline." Keep it simple, no need to demand more than he was willing to give. "Welcome to Montana."

"Where's Dad?"

"Outside still."

Cade's eyes weren't a little bit like their father's—they were exactly like their father's, but the rest of his face bore little resemblance. "Have you had a chance to open any Christmas presents today?"

He nodded. "I got a new phone from Mom." He pulled a phone from the pocket of his baggy trousers. "She sent me a photo of Bo. He's our dog." He turned the phone around to show her a little terrier of some sort, cute as a button. "And Dad got me a watch but it's too big for me to wear so he put it in the safe before we left."

Expensive jewelry for a child. It sounded familiar. "You like dogs? Because we have a friend coming over later who races sled dogs. I don't know if he's coming by sled or by car but they're great fun to be around. They get so excited to mush." Not that he'd get the opportunity to meet them if their father chose to leave. Cade and Rebecca would doubtless go with him. "I have a gift for you." She had more than one but reached for the smallest, *thank you, Rowan, for the suggestion*, and handed it to him. "I think it might go with your phone."

He took it awkwardly and made no move to open it. "I didn't bring you anything."

"But you're here, and it's very nice to meet you. Go

ahead, open it."

He did, while Claire's ponies nibbled at the paper.

"It prints out little photos once you attach it to your phone. It can print out that one of Bo."

"Thank you." Impeccable manners and anxious eyes. He glanced toward the entrance.

Been there, done that, she thought wryly. *I know who you're looking for, and I hope he's a better parent to you than he ever was to me.*

"You have a lot of cowboys," Cade said, and she nodded, because, yes, yes she did. Put five Casey brothers in a room and the testosterone quota went through the roof.

"They're all brothers," she told him confidentially. "That one over there is mine and the one standing next to him belongs to Claire here."

"Can I take a picture of you? Mum said she's always wanted to know what you looked like and you're so pretty. She's pretty, too."

"Have you ever taken a selfie?"

He shook his head no.

"Here, can I borrow your phone?"

He handed it to her reluctantly and she was sure to keep it out of Claire's orbit as she held it up and leaned in close. "It's this round thing here, and... there we are. Can I have one with you? I'll hold it and you press and then you can send it to your mom and then print me a copy and that can be my Christmas present and we can put it on the tree."

Selfish of her, but she wanted this tiny reminder of family, even if she was only a peripheral part of it.

And then Rowan came over and showed Cade how to set up the Polaroid printer, making sure he did all the steps, and then the photo of the two of them appeared and then he printed out the picture of his little dog and propped that up in a lower tree branch too and then he took a picture of the tree and then Bette said, "Hey, kid. I'm as beautiful today as I'm ever going to get, come and take a picture of me sitting on the sofa." And with a quick smile for her and Rowan both, he dashed away to do her bidding.

At which point Madeline flung her arms around Rowan to hide her happy tears. "Good suggestion," she murmured. "*Great* suggestion. You rock. I love this family."

And Rowan hugged back, surprisingly strong. "Good, because you're one of us now and we are here for you."

"The food's ready to go on the table." Cara emerged from the kitchen and she should have looked ridiculous in her borrowed clothes and denim apron with bright orange pom-poms around the edges, but instead, she looked comfortable and altogether happy about it. "Who's going to help carry it?"

Five Casey cowboys headed for the kitchen as a small boy with wide eyes watched them go.

The food came out and Madeline began allocating seats. It seemed only fair to put Savannah at one end of the table, seeing as she'd shelved her own Christmas table plans in order to put her family at Madeline's disposal.

And then the room fell awkwardly quiet as her father entered and stopped abruptly at the room full of people and a table set for plenty. His silvery gaze moved from the picture windows to the tree that took pride of place. He studied the fire blazing merrily and the deep paint colors on the walls not made out of stone. She saw the moment he saw her mother's portrait, and he studied it a moment before turning away.

"I like what you've done with the place," he said, and it was a start.

"Everyone, this is my father, Jonas. Dad, I'll put you and Rebecca and Cade somewhere in the middle of the table, pick a seat and they can sit either side of you. Afterward, if you decide to stay, I'll show you to your rooms." She was running out of rooms. She'd figure it out later.

Chairs scraped as everybody eventually found a place to sit. Madeline dimmed dining sconces just a little and with the flick of a switch turned the Christmas lights on, and it was all she'd ever imagined and more. So much love and goodwill raining down on her as she took her seat opposite Savannah, way down at the other end of the table.

She sat for a moment simply taking it all in and then her gaze landed on the portraits of her mother and grandma Peggy. They were here too, former custodians of this beautiful, nurturing place she now called home.

Hospitality had been important to them.

And as cobbled together as this feast and the people around the table had been, hospitality was important to her too.

She stood abruptly, the scraping of her chair drawing all eyes toward her. Too late to check if her lipstick was perfect or her hair was out of place. Too late to smooth any creases from her beautiful red dress.

Did she start with, *May I have your attention?* when she already had it?

Own your situation, Madeline. Thank you, psychologist number two, because this was her, owning this moment, committing it to beloved memory, throwing her heart wide open to embrace it, safe in the bright, steadying regard of the man at her side.

"I'd like to extend to each and every one of you a warm welcome to my home." Her Swiss finishing school would be proud. "To everyone who's traveled across the country to be here with me today, thank you. And to those of you who didn't have to travel many miles at all but who brought with you the most beautiful gift of acceptance and inclusion, I'm grateful. I'll take good care of your son"—she met Savannah's steady gaze—"your brother"—she sought out all those other Casey cowboy gazes, too—"I won't let Seth down and I'm sure not thinking of ever letting him go."

Laughter came then, and with it a final burst of confidence. "Having you all here this Christmas—every one of you—makes this hands-down the best Christmas I've ever had. Thank you for coming. And with all the love and goodwill in the world, Merry Christmas."

"Hear. Hear."

"Merry Christmas."

"Amen."

She took her seat and blew out a breath as someone passed the beans, and the bread, and the mashed potatoes and gravy. Mason, and Cal started carving turkey and ham. Cara and Symonds tended to the water and the wine.

This day. These people. This beautiful home and valley with wild mountains in the distance.

Seth at her side.

"How did everything get so perfect?" she murmured.

Because it was.

Seth winked at Cade sitting opposite him. "I can answer that."

"Let me guess," offered Cara dryly, as she filled Cade's water glass. "She met you?"

Seth smiled, Cheshire-cat style. "True, but not the answer I have in mind."

"You make houses really pretty?" offered Cade, and made her smile. It wasn't always fun being the offspring of Jonas Love, and she had a whole lot of support to offer if he wanted it. She wanted to be part of this little boy's future.

Seth nodded. "She makes them feel like home. Still not the answer."

Madeline was perfectly willing to let him shoot down her

answer too. "I have a really nice cattle ranch?"

"It's not *that* nice." It wasn't fair that he could melt her with a glance. "I'd call it mediocre at best. Who'd want it? Not me."

Such a performance artist. Madeline looked forward to many more performances from this man she loved without reservation.

A loyal, kind, sexy concrete cowboy who for some reason loved Madeline just the way she was and wasn't shy about letting everyone know it. "Okay, cowboy. Tell us why my day is so perfect."

He lifted her hand to his lips and pressed a kiss to her knuckles. "It's because no matter how hard the challenge, you show up for it with a heart full of hope and determination. And you *try*."

The End

Want more? Check out Jet Casey's story in
Must Love Babies!

Join Tule Publishing's newsletter for more great reads and
weekly deals!

If you enjoyed *Must Love Christmas,*
you'll love the other books in...

The Montana Bachelors and Babies series

Book 1: *Must Love Babies*

Book 2: *Must Love Cowboys*

Book 3: *Must Love Christmas*

Available now at your favorite online retailer!

More books by Kelly Hunter

Maggie's Run
The Outback Brides series

Emma
The Outback Brides of Wirralong series

Matilda Next Door
The Outback Brides Return to Wirralong series

The Jackson Brothers series

Book 1: *The Courage of Eli Jackson*

Book 2: *The Heart of Caleb Jackson*

Book 3: *The Downfall of Cutter Jackson*

Available now at your favorite online retailer!

About the Author

Accidently educated in the sciences, **Kelly Hunter** didn't think to start writing romances until she was surrounded by the jungles of Malaysia for a year and didn't have anything to read. Kelly now lives in Australia, surrounded by lush farmland and family. Kelly is a USA Today bestselling author, a three-time RITA finalist and loves writing to the short contemporary romance form.

Thank you for reading

Must Love Christmas

If you enjoyed this book, you can find more from all our great authors at TulePublishing.com, or from your favorite online retailer.

TULE
PUBLISHING

Made in the USA
Columbia, SC
11 July 2022